THERE IS ALWAYS MORE TO SAY

LYNDA YOUNG SPIRO

Published by New Generation Publishing in 2016

Copyright © Lynda Young Spiro 2016

First Edition

The author asserts the moral right under the Copyright, Designs and Patents Act 1988 to be identified as the author of this work.

All Rights reserved. No part of this publication may be reproduced, stored in a retrieval system or transmitted, in any form or by any means without the prior consent of the author, nor be otherwise circulated in any form of binding or cover other than that which it is published and without a similar condition being imposed on the subsequent purchaser.

This is a work of fiction. Names, characters, businesses, places, events and incidents are either the products of the author's imagination or used in a fictitious manner. Any resemblance to actual persons, living or dead, or actual events is purely coincidental and not intended by the author. Of course you know what they say about good intentions….

www.newgeneration-publishing.com

Printed and bound in Great Britain by
Marston Book Services Ltd, Oxfordshire

For You

"The meeting of two personalities is like the contact of two chemical substances. If there is any reaction, both are transformed."

– C G Jung

Neither will ever be the same again.

"There is nothing to writing. All you do is sit down at a typewriter and bleed."
– Ernest Hemingway

MONDAY 27 OCTOBER, 2014

I feel compelled to write this story. I don't know the ending yet and I can't remember the beginning. Full of the unexpected. Like life itself. This is the story of you and me. This is our story. It began over thirty years ago. It doesn't feel that long ago and only as I sit down to type do I begin to comprehend the length, depth and enormity of its existence. I have tears rolling down my cheeks and I don't know why. I am fifty-five years old.

I often tell people that I have lived and experienced two very different lives. The first being the one before my father died when I was twenty-seven and single. The second being the one that began when I was twenty-eight and married. The married life being the one that I am living now. I have only just realised that these two numbers add up to fifty-five.

And you, my dear friend, are one of the very few to have crossed over between these two lives. You are one of the very few people to have known me during these two different periods of my life. You are one of the very few to have known me before and since my father's death. This story brings these two separate lives of mine together. You who are not in my every day life. But who are often in my thoughts. You have brought these two separate lives of mine together.

It can at times feel like living on two parallel lines. It can at times feel like leading two parallel lives. There is day-to-day life whereby I get up, go to work, meet up with friends. They ask me how I am and I say I'm fine. But then I have my private pain, which is forever, every day, all the time. Tell me this is the same for everyone? I am sure it is.

The truth is always there. Waiting, hidden, somewhere in your mind. If you tell the truth, you don't have to remember anything. But the truth is a matter of one's perspective. This means that not only will different people see the truth differently, but also that the truth itself may vary from person to person. There are glimpses that I can recall. This is my selection of the truth.

Apparently thirty years ago I had said that one day in the future I was going to write a book. I had forgotten. But you of course had remembered. Why have you reminded me of that idle threat made all those years ago? That forgotten flippant remark. Spoken during a conversation from the time when I was living a different life. Why have you come back to me now? Is it to allow all those buried feelings and memories to resurface? Why are you encouraging me to write? Is it because you want me to write this story? I have so many questions. Always. But you already know that.

HEY GIRLIE,
WHY HAVE I ENCOURAGED YOU TO WRITE? BECAUSE YOU SAID YOU WOULD ALL THOSE YEARS AGO. WHY HAVE I COME BACK TO YOU NOW? BECAUSE I NEVER LEFT.
XX

Your recent words have given me time to reflect. I am glad of your encouragement. You have said that I am more than capable of telling a story and I am beginning to think that you may be right. And besides now I have one to tell. You asked me then and you asked me again recently to include you. I am not sure that this is the story you meant me to write. But it's the one I want to tell. A story I have to say that has no ending. But I do not apologise for that. You have dipped in and out of my life over the last thirty years. Thirty years later this story is about us.

Why have you come back into my life? For what reason? To show me what I have been missing all these years? I ask myself. How is it possible that a feeling can remain so powerful over such a long period? The actual amount of time spent together having been so brief. And so long ago. I have no answers. The communication also having always been so sporadic. But the feeling? The feeling is always there. As are the memories. Both the feeling and the memories are so intense. You asked me all those years ago to include you in my story. I am not just telling a story. I am inside this one. So are you. There are always different versions of the same story. This is a short story about a long friendship. This is a story about you and me. Sometimes I wonder if my memories are real or fictional. Sometimes I forget who I am. This is how I see it. This is my reality.

The future is now the present. There was no story then. There is now. Although neither of us know the ending. I write as I speak. I bare my soul.

"There is no unique picture of reality."
— Steven Hawking

"At times you have to leave the city of your comfort and go into the wilderness of your intuition. What you'll discover will be wonderful. What you'll discover is yourself."

– Alan Alda

MAY 1984

I had recently returned from travelling and was at a junction in my life. Before setting off on my three-month trip I had resigned from my job. The relief had been immense. The sense of freedom enormous. I had been unsure as to whether the career path I had originally chosen and had started was the one I wanted to continue. I was uncertain this was the actual route I wanted to follow for my entire working life. Business administration. I was managing an independent travel agency. Developing strategies to hit or exceed sales targets so that the company remained stable and continued to grow. I was twenty-five years old and I wanted to be travelling, not working in an office. It left me feeling cold. Uncreative and unimaginative.

Seven months earlier, in October 1983, my life had been turned upside down. My father had been diagnosed with and treated for lung cancer. He had been forty-eight at the time. He did not smoke. On the day that my father went into remission I resigned from my job. My father's illness had taught me that life is unpredictable. That life is precious. And that opportunities should not be wasted. That we don't know what is around the corner. That life is to be lived. Because you never know when it's going to be taken away. Two weeks after resigning from my job I had boarded a plane to Africa. Finally. To discover another continent. I had wanted to remove myself from my environment. To travel. To find out whom I really was. To find out what I really wanted. From both myself and life itself.

Now that I was back in London I had a lot of decisions to make. Did I even want to stay? Where did I want to go? What did I want to do? What was I looking for? But for the time being I was in London and I knew that I needed to find a job as soon as possible. The money I earned would enable me to move forward with any decisions I was going to make. I knew that any decisions I made would cost me money. I had already learned the importance and power of earning and needed to maintain the financial independence I had enjoyed before I had left. I had just turned twenty-five.

I had taken a job that I had seen advertised. I remember recognising the fact that there had been potential for both overtime and tips in the advert. I had liked the advert and it had caught my attention. The hours were long but it was shift work. Working a six-day fortnight appealed to me. I would have time to reacquaint myself with my city, with my family and with my friends. Somehow—and I am not quite sure why—the advert had sounded exotic.

What could be less exotic than working in a traditional British café in the middle of Soho? Except The Soho Café was different to your usual greasy spoon. It was greasy spoon meets Soho Bohemian. It might not have been exotic but it was authentic. Old advertisements for groceries from the early part of the last century adorned the walls. The tables were covered in red and white checked tablecloths. They were the wipeable plastic type whereupon we used to place the simple food devoid of frills.

The café had its own charm. The type of charm that doesn't exist in today's restaurant chains. The same chains that seem to have replaced cafés similar to this particular one. The clients were an eclectic mixture of locals and media types. There were the couples who came in at lunch time, who were obviously having affairs. Office affairs. They would sit cosied up in the far corner. Giggling. Occasionally kissing. Holding hands. Behaving like young lovers. To us they had appeared old. We used to laugh about them in amazement. About their age and what they were getting up to. They were probably only in their late thirties or early forties. What was old then is young now.

And then there were the media types. The men who worked in one of the film companies or advertising agencies that lined Wardour Street on both sides.

Scattered amongst the many Chinese restaurants. They would shout loudly for all to hear about their latest conquest. A recognised achievement at work. Of a sort. From the starlet to the older divorced woman who worked in the accounts department. It didn't matter who it was. As long as it was their success. Whilst their wives remained at home. Now bringing up the children. After having given up their own careers. Oblivious to their husband's daytime shenanigans.

The Soho Café was full of both character and characters. It emanated a very relaxed atmosphere full of warmth and happiness. It was homely. It was friendly. There was a wonderful ambience evident which was tangible upon entry. The door was kept closed to hang on to that magical atmosphere. To keep it contained. And it was here in The Soho Café we met.

I don't remember much about those times we spent together during 1984. My memories are rather vague. But I do remember them as being the happiest of times and incredibly special. Plenty of work and even more play. It was hard to differentiate between the two. The one spilling over into the other.

I don't even remember the exact date when we met but I do remember where we were. I also remember that I had just turned twenty-five. My memories of meeting you are fading but not the feeling. An inexplicable feeling I would never experience again. I had never met anyone like you before. I haven't since. Your beautiful blue eyes. That seductive smile and the way you said my name. Your voice. Your American accent. That particularly distinctive and casual drawl. Your body. So lean. So slender. So athletic. The way you wore your clothes. The clothes you wore. Your drainpipe jeans and your well-cut jackets. Your black or white T-shirt and your Converse trainers. *Shall I go on?*

The way you moved. The way you moved me. Your haircut, short, sharp, sleek. Your dark blonde hair slightly sun bleached. In another life you could have been a hairdresser. Your skin so bronzed. So smooth to the touch. So soft. The nape of your neck. The sound of your laughter. So intoxicating. I remember that you always made me feel happy. That I loved spending time with you. That we shared and enjoyed a level of intimacy that I took for granted. Being together made me happy. We were most certainly an interesting couple. Life was good. It was uncomplicated. Or so I had thought. But you hadn't told me yet. Could things have worked out any differently? Who knows? Were we ahead of our time? Born a generation too soon. Or just two young conformists? Doing what was expected of us. There are so many questions and so few answers.

I have already mentioned I cannot remember exactly when we first met although that isn't completely true.

I have been trying for so long now to remember the moment of our meeting. I cannot remember it and I cannot reinvent it. But I need to correct myself. I do remember when I first saw you. It was a revelation. As I saw you walking across The Soho Café. Towards me. And when our eyes first met. It was so powerful. I was locked in. From the beginning. As were you. The first time I set eyes on you I felt a deep connection. As if I had always known you. From another life. That sense of recognition. The feeling always there. The feeling always the same. The immediate knowledge that we will always be together. If not in this life then in the next. But I don't remember when we first spoke. I know we met by chance. The randomness of fate. We found each other by pure serendipity. People come into your life when you are least expecting them. That I know is true.

Why is it that I forget key moments in my life? Why do some memories escape me completely and why are others so faded? Why can't I recollect such happy times in my life? Such as meeting you. I wonder if your memories are the same as mine. Probably not. That doesn't mean better or worse. Just different.

The café was run by an adorable Italian who was called Carlo. We used to laugh about what he must have been like in his youth. Do you remember that? Carlo who had inherited the café from his father Mario. Carlo taught us kids the importance of a work ethic. But then we must have had that ethic already seeing as we had individually and independently responded to one of his adverts. Like minded twenty somethings.

And you. You were one of the waiting staff. And I was another. We worked on opposite shifts. You had come from the United States to the United Kingdom. To work and travel and discover the world. You had left your job. Knowing that you didn't want to be an engineer for the rest of your life, but realising that you knew no more than that. You had left behind your two great loves: your surfboard and the Pacific Ocean. You had brought your camera. To capture your experiences. You had said goodbye to your friends and your family. You had left your life in Malibu, a beach city, not far from Los Angeles. To find yourself. I don't think you found yourself at all. I think you found me instead. The day I swapped shifts with Charlie was the day that changed my life. And yours as well I think.

What did we do whilst at work? We did almost everything. And most certainly anything that was asked of us. Almost everything that is apart from the cooking. Carlo's wife Maria did the cooking amongst other chores. Maria was a saint. She understood Carlo and he understood her. They were a real team. And perfect teachers. They taught us well but we were eager to learn. They taught us the meaning of both hard work and teamwork. We worked as a team.

At any one time there were only six members of staff in the café and that would include Carlo and Maria who were always there. They lived in the flat above and so even when Maria could slip away, she wasn't very far. We were shift workers. Collectively the four waiting staff on both shifts were known as 'The Fab Four'. Once you and I started working together we became known as 'The Dynamic Duo'.

I remember occasionally we were allowed to make the cappuccinos under the watchful eye of Carlo and the guidance of Maria. But that was after 6pm when the café had closed for the day. Before the coffee machine was cleaned by Carlo. To this day I make an almost perfect cappuccino. The secret is to heat the cup up first.

On the whole the job was to support Carlo and Maria in the smooth and efficient running of the café. And that is what we did, to the best of our ability. Learning along the way. Between us we would prepare and lay the tables, always making sure that they were clean and tidy. We would greet the customers in a friendly but most courteous manner, give out the menus and then advise on menu choices. That was the fun part. Familiarising ourselves with the menu so as to be able to assist customers in their choice. We would take the orders for the food and drink. We served the meals. We cleared and tidied the tables and dealt with the cash payments. We would replenish the salt cellars and the pepper grinders and refill the ketchup and brown sauce bottles. We would fold the napkins. We waited on the customers and helped to create and contribute to the friendly and welcoming atmosphere.

It was a busy environment. The hours were long and the work was physically exhausting. The café was open seven days a week from 8am to 6pm. We started at 6am and finished at 8pm. Even though we worked hard and the hours were long we had plenty of time to play, considering we only worked six days out of every fortnight.

Every day was different. The people I met. The customers. They were the ones who made the job so enjoyable for me. There were very few tourists. Although once a couple from Malibu came in, and I saw that far away look in your eyes when you spoke about the sea and your love of surfing. The regulars who we got to know used to come and tell us their stories. The working girls would always come in first for a hearty breakfast. The ladies of the night. They would laugh amongst themselves about their previous night's clients. They never ceased to entertain us whilst regaling their stories. Everyone had their own story. Some were interesting and others were less so. Each one was different. Some people had more than one. Everybody had a story to tell although not everyone told theirs.

An integral part of the job was to make sure that the

customers enjoyed their experience. We were always on hand to answer any questions. They invariably weren't about the menu either. The customers were interested in us, and whilst we served them food they fed us with stories of their life experiences.

Here too, I knew that I could continue to remain anonymous and just be me. The *me* who I had begun to learn about whilst I had been away from home. The *me* who I wanted to be, not just the person I was expected to be. I was taking advantage of being back in London. Here in The Soho Café I knew that I could continue my journey even though I was back home. I loved that I was seeing another side of life in London. A completely different type of work environment, and meeting people from totally different walks of life.

And you. You were just starting out on your adventure. Beginning your journey. But somehow—and I don't know how this happened—you had packed your bags badly before you had left home. You had brought baggage with you that maybe should have been left behind. The rest was to follow you. But I didn't know that yet. *You did.*

"Choose a job you love, and you will never have to work a day in your life."
– Confucius

"Really important meetings are planned by the souls long before the bodies see each other."
– Paulo Coelho

FRIDAY 6 JUNE, 2014

I have always loved receiving post. I still do. When I was a child I would listen out for the thud of letters onto the hall mat, and I would charge down the stairs to see if there was anything for me. Invariably there wasn't, but on those rare occasions when there was something for me, well those were the best days. The most memorable days. A postcard from my French pen pal. Or news from my grandparents who used to escape to Spain to avoid the foggy winters of my childhood in London. Birthday cards, Christmas cards and the occasional Valentine's card. I feel no differently about receiving emails today. The anticipation of what has been written. The excitement of what is about to be read. What the email will reveal to me. To this day I still love receiving post. There is always that same sense of excitement.

Obviously, I was thrilled when out of the blue on a rather ordinary summer's day back in June, I received an email from you. I smiled. Just seeing your name. And as always that feeling. We hadn't had any contact for rather a long time, which wasn't unusual at all. That's just the way it was. The way it had always been. Over the last thirty years since we had met at The Soho Café in 1984, our communication had been somewhat infrequent, to say the least. But we had kept each other updated with almost annual correspondence in one form or another. Intense periods followed by periods of drought. Occasional postcards, letters and even I remember a series of impassioned phone calls after your visit in 1994. But more about that later.

Methods of communication had changed over the years, but never the feeling. As time went by and technology advanced we progressed from postcards, letters, texts, and even to the occasional email. Only the feeling remained the same, which made the content more powerful even if it seemed so simple. But always better still was the very rare but cherished phone call. There was something about your voice. Or was it what you said to me? What is the glue that has kept us stuck together throughout these years?

Where had the years gone? What had we been doing? As you said later we had both spent the time building our lives. Occasionally, I had the feeling that my foundation block was missing. At times my palace crumbled and then it would strengthen again. Up and down like the waves in the sea that you were surfing back home.

Your timing is impeccable, as is your sense of style I remember. It was probably about eighteen months since we had last enjoyed any meaningful contact and before that possibly two years. I hadn't forgotten that your son was living and working in London. Although it was a fact I had been trying to ignore for the last eighteen months. You had told me that he would be coming after the London Olympics in 2012. That he would be coming for two years and that you would come over then and so I would see you sometime. I remember laughing because you had said that you might be old and grey by then. At least we will have both aged you had said.

I couldn't wait to open the email, which obviously I did immediately. And then I read it.

HEY GIRLIE,
I'LL BE IN LONDON FROM THE 1ST TO THE 11TH SEPTEMBER. WILL YOU BE AROUND FOR A CUPPA OR SOMETHING?
XX

The phone rings and I return to reality. You have always had the ability to take me to another place. My mind had drifted to the last time we had met. 1994. Twenty years ago. Where had the time gone? The truth is I haven't thought about you daily for the last twenty years. When I do think of you it's so profound. I couldn't think of you all the time. I remember what happened after that visit. So much to tell you. So many questions. Face to face, I want to look you in the eye and tell you. Tell you everything. If I can.

Through the window I see a pair of butterflies dancing in the sun. Flirting with each other. Whenever I see a butterfly I think of you. Possibly because of the feeling. The fluttering of their wings. Like the flutter in my heart. I have a book that says: 'If you dream of this beautiful insect you will find success in love and friendship.' The butterfly is a symbol of transformation because of its impressive process of metamorphosis. That out of bad maybe something good will come? What are you trying to tell me? I know you are with me always. Spiritually by my side. I have waited so long for this moment. I knew you would come back one day. It was only a matter of time. Twenty years. I can barely breathe in anticipation.

Outside in the sunshine the butterflies are continuing their dance amongst the sweet peas. I try to imagine what life as a butterfly would be like. My whole life changing to such an extreme that I would be unrecognisable at the end of the transformation. Unquestionably, the butterfly embraces the changes of her environment and her body. If only it were so easy to accept the changes in our lives as casually as she does. I realise the phone has stopped ringing.

I believe people come into your life for a reason and at certain times. Be that good or bad. Some people are transient. Some are forever. Forever can mean with many years of no contact. I am beginning to wonder why you have come back into my life. My day-to-day life is generally good. I am beginning to wonder for what reason you are returning. People come back into your life when you are least expecting them. That I know is true. I reply to your email.

YOU BET! X

I can't wait to see you. The absolute sheer delight I feel at the prospect of seeing you again after all this time. It's been so long. Twenty years. A lifetime away. Although it feels like yesterday.

My husband says I tell him everything that I want him to know. He doesn't question me. He is right. I tell him what I want him to know. I hide some things. I hide you. I don't know why I hide you.

But Alex. I have to tell Alex. The one person who knows you. *Remember Alex?* Of course you do. And Alex remembers you. Nothing is hidden from Alex. The one person whom I have allowed and actively encouraged to remember you. Alex the person who knows me better than I know myself.

"When a butterfly flutters its wings in one part of the world, it can eventually cause a hurricane in another."
– Edward Norton Lorenz

"Each friend represents a world in us, a world not born until they arrive, and it is only by this meeting that a new world is born."

– Anais Nin

MAY 1984

Alex and I had met in 1974. Ten years earlier. We had found each other when we were fifteen years old, and neither of us have wanted to let go nor look back since. We who were so different. Right from the beginning. Alex and I are connected as only fifteen-year-old best friends can be. Sometimes I think that my sense of humour is quite underdeveloped when I am with Alex. What made us laugh when we were fifteen, still makes us laugh today. The very striking Alex. Lovely, clever, good looking, wise and charming Alex. Sharp-eyed Alex. Raven-haired Alex. Fair-skinned Alex. The both beautiful and handsome Alex. The effortlessly seductive Alex. Alex the one who everybody fell in love with. A person not easily forgotten.

Since college days Alex and I had lived together. In the beginning we had shared a house with four others. A mixed household. Three boys and three girls. All of us students. None of us studying the same subject. A diverse group of people. The first time away from home for all of us. Here Alex and I had learned to cook and clean and look after ourselves and each other.

Once our student days were over, we both found work and moved from the student house and shared a flat. Just the two of us. The lovely flat where we were living today. The flat was on the ground floor of an impressive Georgian semi-detached house, which in itself was set on a beautiful tree-lined terrace. It was in a popular and leafy residential area on the north-west side of London and was within cycling distance to the West End. I loved the ride through the peaceful and green outer circle of Regent's Park, both at the beginning and end of each work day. For the last couple of years Alex and I had been living in total happiness in our beautiful two-bedroomed flat. We were both very lucky to be able to live here and we knew it. We both paid a minimal rent. The flat was owned by Alex's father.

And it was here in this lovely flat of mine and Alex that you and I would spend most of our time together. Alex and I loved living there. We had decorated our bedrooms to our own very individual, different and distinctive tastes. Alex's room was all muted with subtle colours. Mine was colourful and bright. And loud with a jukebox in it. Colourful, bright and loud. A reflection of both myself and my life. We decorated the lounge to suit both of our tastes. Wooden floors and futons, which later were replaced by Chesterfield settees. Or was it the other way round, I can't remember? But it was in this lounge, the hub of the flat, where the wonderfully entertaining gatherings would take place most nights of the week after work and often on the weekends too. Everyone had such fun in that flat. That's the sort of place it was. The lounge could have been full of the most interesting assortment of people, but when you were there amongst them, the only person I ever saw was you. I can't begin to describe the secrets that were contained within those four walls. It feels like a breach of trust repeating some of those stories. Even to you. You were welcomed into our home. You were a pleasure to have around and fitted in perfectly. Like a well-fitting glove.

Soon after we met at The Soho Café you became an almost permanent fixture in the flat that Alex and I shared together. You and I enjoyed many candlelit dinners during our months together as a couple. I enjoyed cooking. I enjoyed cooking for you. Cooking uses all the senses. Experimenting with food. And entertaining you. I can't remember what I used to cook in particular. The meals that stay in my mind are not the good ones. Or should I say not the kind of meals that would be remembered for the food that was eaten. The importance for me has always been about the people who are there. I have enjoyed some of my favourite meals with you. Even the one that will always be known as 'The Last Supper'. I can't remember what I cooked on that particular occasion. It's not relevant. But I do remember that over dinner we shared secrets and stories and I ate them up along with my food. And when my stomach was full, my appetite for you was far from sated. My appetite for you was insatiable. You shared your biggest secret with me during that meal. A secret I would never have guessed. A secret I would rather not have known. You told me you were engaged to be married. That we could never be together. That your partner would be joining you in London in a few months time. I don't remember what I felt when you told me. But I can remember the look of sadness in your eyes. I am now your secret.

Apparently I came into your life about a month after you had written that letter. Not very long after your arrival in England. Which particular letter was that? I can only assume it was the one describing your loneliness during your first and only winter in London. The letter you had sent not long after your arrival in the United Kingdom. When you were still living in the youth hostel in Bayswater. Before you had found your flat. And before you had found me at The Soho Café where we both worked. But on opposite shifts. Only meeting when I subsequently swapped shifts for a day with Charlie. As a favour for Charlie. We met by chance. I came into your life about a month after you had written that letter in which you had proposed to your partner Ashley.

Were you missing the beach, the warm weather, the sea and of course the surf? Did you know what you were letting yourself in for before you came to London? Weather wise I mean. I thought about that afterwards. What inspired you to write that letter in which you proposed? Was it because you missed Malibu, your family and your friends. Your other life. The life you had chosen to leave behind once you had boarded that plane to London from Los Angeles. I don't think I have ever asked you. And if I have, I don't remember the answer. Perhaps you were in love? I think that it would be an inappropriate question for me to ask maybe.

Later you told me that over the years during your dating period you had been unceremoniously dumped a few times by Ashley. And I had said that everyone needs to feel rejection at some point in their life because everyone needs to feel that pain. We grow from that pain. Rejection can make you more determined to prove your abilities. To sharpen your competitiveness. To give you an incentive to prove people wrong. Had you yourself even made your own mind up as to what you wanted? Did you really know then? That you wanted to be with Ashley for the rest of your life. Or were you doing what was expected of you? We are from such differing backgrounds and yet we share this bond. You are a dreamer. A hugely passionate and artistic person. Maybe you are the anomaly in your family as I am in mine. Perhaps that is why we found each other. What were you looking for when you found me? You were definitely searching for something. Or was it someone you were looking for? On and off you and Ashley had been together for around six years when you wrote that letter in which you proposed.

I was twenty-five years old and you were a mere twenty-three. The ages that our children are today. The children that we both have with our respective day-to-day life partners.

"What is that you express in your eyes? It seems to me more than all the print I have read in my life."
— Walt Whitman

"Be courteous to all, but intimate with few, and let those few be well tried before you give them your confidence."

– George Washington

SUNDAY 8 JUNE, 2014

Alex and I meet almost every Sunday. This week I have some exciting news which I want to share. Only with Alex. My oldest and closest friend of forty years. My friend. The one who knows me better than I know myself. Alex who I trust more than anyone. Alex who understands me more than anyone. Alex who all those years ago taught me the true meaning of unconditional love. Through sickness and in health. The person who knows and understands me best. We have seen each other through the bad times and share the good ones together. And it is during these times that our friendship has evolved and worked. We have enjoyed and continue to enjoy separate experiences. Ours is a friendship that has surpassed all others. Our friendship is warm and loving and deep. It is an intimate and affectionate relationship. Our friendship has never been marred by a sexual attraction. By neither of us. We have moved from teenagers to the threshold of adulthood and beyond. Through marriages, births, deaths, sickness and of course the challenges of every day life. Over the years we have never quarreled or competed and as other relationships flourish and die, we are always there for each other, travelling from coast to coast through the most tumultuous times. We are lucky to have each other.

This morning, sitting with Alex in my garden, we spoke about you. I told Alex that I would be seeing you for the first time in twenty years. That I had received an email from you two days earlier to say you were finally returning to London. And that I was so excited. But Alex had already felt my excitement from the moment I had opened the front door. And Alex was excited for me. Well, for us actually. We sat outside my bedroom on the stone bench I had bought at the local garden centre all those years ago. When we first moved into this flat. Our family home. And I am looking at the camellia tree. The buds on the branches opening ever so slightly, a little more each day until they will bloom in their entirety and then die until the following spring. Then the whole process will start all over again. The camellia tree that I had lovingly dug up and removed from the garden of my childhood home before my mother had completed on the sale of the house. I had uprooted a section of the enormous bush and replanted it in the home that I shared with my husband and children. And ten years later by the time the tree had re-established itself we sold that house and chose to move to a ground-floor flat with a garden. The camellia tree was once again uprooted and this time I replanted it outside our bedroom. And this is where Alex and I are now sitting. Thinking. Remembering. My childhood. My teens. This tree a part of my earlier life. My formative years.

Your recent email has given me time to reflect over the last thirty years since we met. Not only am I thinking about the happy times we spent together, and my goodness there were happy times. Plenty of them. I cannot remember any grey days when you were around. Even though there probably were but either I never noticed or I don't remember them. My memories are filled with sunshine. There's something very lovely about digging deep into my memory and searching for and retrieving memories from events that have happened in my life.

I enjoy living a colourful life in a colourful world. I always have and always will. Colour expresses emotions and stimulates the senses. It surrounds us. My morning mood determines the visual cacophony of multi-colours that I will wear on any particular day. I like to wear many differently multi-coloured layers of clothing in the hope of evoking these precious but fading memories. I am influenced by the colours that bedeck me. The colours I wear affect my mood. From my socks upwards. And my shoes. Colour makes me feel happy. It really is as simple as that. I don't understand why so many people wear black and envelope themselves in such darkness. Wearing black can influence my mood and make me feel sad, although I like my underwear to be black. Black underwear makes me feel strong and powerful.

It also looks marginally better. I don't know why I am writing this.

Today I am wearing a jacket that I bought seventeen years ago. I keep everything that is important to me. I like to be surrounded by aesthetically pleasing works of art. Be they paintings, ceramics or textiles. I derive pleasure as well as inspiration from these objects of beauty and colour. My most treasured possessions being every crumbling fraying piece of embroidery, stuffed toy, papier-mâché, clay or painting my children have both made and brought home from school. But you are my object of desire. Even now after all these years. These thoughts. Remembering. A long way away. And another life. The lovely past.

But not all my memories from the last thirty years are good ones. It isn't just you who I think about. Often as I try to recollect certain events in my life different memories come to the surface. Different situations and different circumstances. Thoughts even. About my day-to-day life also.

And now as we sit here laughing in the sun and reminiscing, Alex has told me that I should really be writing this story down exactly as I am telling it now. Alex tells me that our story—yours and mine—should be the subject of a book. Alex thinks it's a lovely story and that people will enjoy reading it. Alex has got me thinking. I find the idea both enchanting and exciting.

"Memory is the diary that we all carry about with us."

– Oscar Wilde

"You have your way. I have my way. As for the right way, the correct way, and the only way, it does not exist."

– Friedrich Nietzche

OCTOBER 1984–DECEMBER 1985

From the moment we met at The Soho Café I recognised that I wanted to be with you. And it didn't overly concern me that you were engaged as I already knew that in reality we could never be together. In another life. Maybe. Your partner Ashley arrived in October 1984, having bought the engagement ring in the Duty Free on the way to London. But that wasn't a surprise to you. It had seemed strange to me. Rather clinical. It had concerned me. I remember quite clearly thinking at the time that I'm sure couples normally do this together. Choose the ring together. A joint decision. In unison. Isn't that what marriage was all about? We both knew that our special friendship—yours and mine—couldn't continue in the same way after Ashley arrived to join you. It hadn't seemed right. The deceit. No that wasn't for me. It felt like an abuse of your vows before you had even taken them. Although in truth that wasn't really my problem. In fact, I can remember soon after your partner Ashley's initial arrival in London I hurled myself into another relationship almost immediately. In front of your eyes. With someone whom you knew and also worked with at The Soho Café. I hadn't wanted to make you hurt. I hope I didn't. But I think I did. It wasn't intentional if I did. I promise you. But it wasn't about you. It was about me. I never asked you what your true innermost feelings and thoughts were about the prospect of being joined in London by your partner, five months after we had met. That's just the way it was.

I had never met anyone like you before. I haven't since. We had spent a blissful few months together. Pursuing the relationship was never an option. Ours was an emotive and evocative relationship whichhad caught us both off guard. There was no going back after the places we had taken each other to. It just goes to show what a huge role chance plays in life. I had never felt passion like this before. Was it because you were my forbidden fruit? I let you go. Although I had no choice. But you were always there.

I have very few memories whatsoever from the times we spent together after your partner Ashley arrived. Ashley was a physiotherapist. Iron-handed. Strong and solid. Like a large rock. Immovable. Impenetrable. Hard and cold. The opposite to you. You are soft and gentle. A warm and caring individual. Ashley has a long face with a strong jaw line. Ashley is controlling, domineering, overbearing. A determined individual. Ashley who has a habit of correcting you is strict and tense. I don't like the harsh manner in which Ashley says your name. You are casual. You are relaxed. You are easy going.

Ashley and you are polar opposites. Ashley is the antithesis of you.

You rather naively thought that we could all be friends. Obviously we couldn't. But we continued to spend time together. Sometimes with your partner and sometimes without. Just the two of us always being our preferred choice. Neither of us wanting to let go. Ashley did not like our friendship. Ashley had deep concerns about our friendship. From the beginning there was a level of suspicion. These feelings were of course both understandable and justifiable. And correct. But nothing was ever confirmed to Ashley. I can remember our rather awkward denial. We began to see less of each other. Knowing, feeling and appreciating each other's pain. Our friendship disrupted. And not long after Ashley's arrival in London we left The Soho Café. You and I. Both of us knowing that it really was time to let go of each other. We both moved on. Well on the surface. I had jumped into a new relationship and you had fallen back into your old one with Ashley.

You and Ashley left to travel around Europe before your return home. That was in May 1985. One year after our chance meeting at The Soho Café where you and I had both been working. But on different shifts. I have often thought about where else we might have met if I hadn't have worked on your shift that day. If I hadn't have agreed to swap with Charlie. But our paths were always going to cross. Somewhere. Of that

I'm sure.

Before setting off on your travels you let go of the lease on your flat. The flat that had originally been for both of us to enjoy but then so quickly became both of yours. I never went back there after Ashley arrived. You used to come to me. Both of you. I remember you weren't in London when I had chicken pox in July 1985. I also remember being incredibly sad that I couldn't go to Live Aid because of the chicken pox. And when you came back from travelling seven months later both you and Ashley came to stay with us in our flat for three weeks before you finally went home for Christmas. I remember nothing about this time. Neither does Alex. But one of the few photos that I have of you was taken in our lounge surrounded by your cases kneeling on the floor. Dated December 1985. Were you praying? And if so, what for?

Thinking back, I don't remember being devastated by your departure at the time. I don't remember your actual leaving, but I do know that you left the UK for the final time homeward bound in December 1985.

And then as quickly as you had come into my life you were gone. And life returned to normal. Whatever normal was or is. I had ended the new relationship I had jumped into so quickly. I had gone into it for all the wrong reasons. My heart wasn't ready for anyone but you. But even so, I was making the most of my single life. Times were fun and rather interesting. And during the cold and dull winter and towards the spring for a few months I lived and enjoyed a full and busy life in a new and different way since you had gone.

We never had the opportunity to give ourselves a chance. I think about that now but never then. We accepted the situation. Or at least I did. I do remember I wasn't the one who was engaged. I wasn't the one whose partner had bought the ring in the Duty Free on the way to London.

Suddenly things began to look decidedly less good. I met you when my dad was in remission. My family only fractured. Not yet broken. When the cancer seemed to have gone away. The only thing to go away was you. My father's cancer had come back. And with a vengeance. Funny how you can forget about something and put it to the back of your mind. Until that ghastly return, which was just two years after the original diagnosis. And this amount of time in the doctor's eyes was longer than anticipated. For me it was a living nightmare.

"Don't be dismayed by good-byes. A farewell is necessary before you can meet again. And meeting again, after moments or lifetimes, is certain for those who are friends."

– Richard Bach

"Death ends a life, not a relationship."
— Mitch Albom

AUGUST 1986

August 1986 was an emotionally charged month for me. It was a time when I met my husband, and within the space of three weeks my grandfather and father died. I remember nothing more about the month of August. I can't remember exactly when I met my husband. I met him during the second week of August in 1986. Just before my paternal grandfather died on August 13. And before my father died on August 29. I can't remember the exact date when I met my husband.

I think you know how I met my husband. I'm sure I've told you. I met my husband at a mutual friend's wedding party. He knew both the bride and groom and had even introduced them to each other. I knew the bride and her brother. I went to the wedding party with the bride's brother. I really hadn't wanted to go out the night I met my husband. I went as a favour for my friend. He hadn't wanted to go to the party alone. The brother of the bride. My husband had come to London for one night only. Just for the wedding party. He was on his way to the States where he would be staying for three weeks. He was then coming back to London for a few days. He was staying with the bride's brother. By the time he had returned to London both my grandfather and my father had died.

Before he died I told my father that I had met the man I was going to marry. It was one of my happiest moments, and I am so glad I was able to tell him. It almost felt as if I was releasing him from his parental responsibilities. That he wouldn't have to worry about me any longer. His slightly wayward and to date unmarried daughter. It felt like I was letting my father go. I knew the night I met my husband that I was going to marry him. I had an epiphany. It was a very special moment when I just knew. I saw it in my head. No, not an actual wedding but us together. I knew that I would be safe with him. I knew that I had met the person who would look after me and take good care of me. Who would love me and cherish me, and who would give me stability. I told my father that my future husband was an accountant. As was my father. My future husband had an earring and a thin plait which wasn't overly noticeable, however, I didn't tell my father.

I am not sure why but I have always felt different. I have always known the feeling of being on the outside. Those feelings of otherness. I don't know how I should or could feel otherwise. This is just the way I am. I know that others feel the same way too. I cannot put a name to this feeling. Do you recognise this feeling? This feeling of just knowing.

I know that people come into your life for a reason and at certain times, but why do people come into your life when you are least expecting them? You never have a choice about what happens to you in life, but you always have a choice about how you deal with it. Pain makes you grow. My father was the person in life who spread joy and love and laughter and wisdom. Thinking about how he lived his life has affected the way I am able to deal with mine in his absence. Today I think about how I live my life because it will affect the way people are able to deal with theirs in my absence.

I have learnt that although my father was taken from me, I know that no one will ever be able to take away my wonderful memories of him. They will stay with me forever. These memories do not fade. I adored and respected my father. He could do no wrong in my eyes. When I was a child and growing up I remember my greatest fear was that my father would die when he was young. I imagined that it would be the worst thing that could ever happen to me. And then it happened. He was fifty-two years old. And I survived.

But my life had ruptured, split and become divided. It had ceased to be what it once had been. Everything changed. I became a different person. My family became broken, and life as I had known it was never the same again.

Every time I hear of someone having lost their father it brings back my own pain. I am damaged by death. I am not frightened by the thought of death. I think it is far worse for those who are left behind. I was there at my grandmother's flat when she was told that my father had died. Her youngest son. I can still hear her primal scream. The pain she would endure for the rest of her life. The loss of her child. I know you survive and continue to live after people die. I experienced my greatest fear at twenty-seven. It has prepared me for most eventualities.

When my father originally became ill in October 1983 my bubble burst. We all hoped and prayed the cancer would leave his body. That it would go away for good. But this sadly never happened. There was a short time when it looked as if it had. A year or so. Maybe. It was during this once again happy time. This period of remission. That I met you in May 1984 at The Soho Café. This is where we had both found work and where we were to find each other. When in June 1986 the cancer eventually returned with a vengeance, I grew up almost overnight. I put my cards on the table and realised that it was game over. I'm not sure I particularly knew what the game was, but I knew that it had come to an end.

Watching my father get weaker as his illness progressed was a brutal lesson in how little control we have over our lives. I recognised the fact that my father was dying. It was more than apparent to me.

My father, the person who had taught me to pick myself up when I fell down, both mentally and physically. The person who taught me the difference between right and wrong. The person who taught me to make time for everyone and to have time for everybody, whoever they were. Before he died I told my father many things I felt I wanted to share with him. I told my father about you. Talking so openly to my father before his death has helped me cope a little more easily. Dealing with bereavement is not about forgetting and moving on. It's about rebuilding trust in life. I have lost my faith over the years. I suppose it started from when my father became ill. I have never lost my faith or trust in you.

After my father died I remember thinking no one would ever love me as much as he had ever again. I felt like my protective force was suddenly missing. I asked my mother if I could have a couple of his sweaters. I knew the two that I wanted. A dark blue wool one from Harrods that smelt of his lovely aftershave. And a pale blue golfing sweater that he had bought whilst on holiday. A family road trip along the Pacific Coast Highway in 1979. The holiday that had begun in Los Angeles and had ended in San Francisco. A great holiday. The best family holiday that I can remember. Before my father's cancer. Before I had met you. Since my father's death twenty-eight years ago, I have kept both of these sweaters close to me. In my bedside cupboard. Hidden away. Like you.

I remember writing you a letter, telling you my thoughts about my father and how I respected him and loved him. There isn't a day that goes by when I don't think of him or want to tell him something. I still have the letter that you wrote back to me. Hidden away amongst my treasures. I don't have to read it to remember what you wrote. Words like that don't get forgotten.

Everybody has moments that are really life changing. In anyone's life there are a small amount of memorable events that will occur, which are never forgotten. In my life it was the loss of my father and the lead up to his death. The day I met my husband was another moment when I entered my new and different life. Another life. A different life from the one I had experienced with you.

Timing is everything. My life changed irrevocably when my father died. When you've been to the depths of despair you see things more clearly. When things like that happen to you in your life, you change. Experiences change you and you change as a person. I learned the fragility of life at a relatively young age. As the pain of loss has given way to memories, I have begun to heal. My father's death has left me changed forever. I often wonder how different things could have been if he were still alive. I have also questioned how different things may have been had you remained in London.

"What you leave behind is not what is engraved in stone monuments, but what is woven into the lives of others."

– Pericles

"What is the good of experience if you do not reflect?"

– Frederick the Great

WEDNESDAY 8 JULY, 2014

It is late afternoon on a beautiful summer's day. I have taken my coffee into the garden and I am admiring the mass of colour. These flowers will continue to bloom I hope, until the first frost arrives. Multi-coloured dahlias of different sizes mixed together. A disorganised array of colour. And then I spot a ladybird. Always mention the ladybird. The little creature who comes to me in times of trouble, who shows me that she cares and that everything will be alright. That this is a journey which at times is most unpleasant but is often filled with joy. The birds are singing and the light is perfect. Bright. It is a warm day. My terrace. One of my favourite places to reminisce. And reflect. From here I can see the greenery of the woods and hear the birds and also smell the flowers. I am looking at the poppies that are in bloom. The flowers that have grown from the seeds I scattered. And it is here in these surroundings today enveloped by nature where I have chosen to reminisce. About what I don't yet know.

I am trying to unearth these memories. It is very hard. For more reasons than one. But they will come. Something always does. That's the way it goes. Whilst digging deep into my soul and retrieving memories, I am learning a lot about the present day me. I am thinking about and remembering the past. My head is all over the place. Scrambled thoughts and memories. What comes to mind first? Jumping from year to year. Where shall I start? My thoughts. I feel like I have an open wound. Never properly healed. Always sore and weeping. Forgive me rambling on and stay with me please. It is important for me whilst digging deeply into my memories that I write them down and remind you of certain occasions, scenarios, magical moments and secrets. I want to tell you about me, about my day-to-day life. I want to hear about you and your day-to-day life. There is so much more I want to know about you. It feels like starting over again. From the beginning. It's exciting.

I have a few good friends. People who I have chosen to keep close to me. I have friends who are both much older and much younger than me. A young person should always have an older friend and an older person should always have a younger friend. To learn from each other. To see the other one's perspective. Because it will be different. One's outlook on life changes with age. I realise that most of the people I mix with in my day-to-day life either know each other or know of each other. *What do they say about six degrees of separation?* That by way of introduction everyone and everything is six or fewer steps away from any other person in the world. But not you. No one knows you. Only I know you. Although I introduced you to my oldest, dearest and closest friend Alex in 1984. I met Alex through a mutual friend in 1974. Coincidentally, almost twelve years later I met my husband through the same mutual friend. That friend said our marriage would never last. I had forgotten this until recently. I don't know how. Perhaps it is because we no longer have contact with this person. None of us. Not me. Definitely not Alex. And not even my husband now.

I have learnt that everyone has a different interpretation of love. We all love people differently. Even the same people. I loved my parents differently to the way my sister does. And they in turn loved us differently. My relationship with my parents was most certainly different to that of my sister's. We were both brought up in the same environment, but each had a very different relationship with both my mother and my father.

I have always loved my parents, my sister, my husband, my children, my friends, Alex and you. And other people at different times in my life. Transient people. But being in love. That loss of control where you can't imagine life without that other person. I have never wanted to feel this. It seems to me impossible to put that responsibility on one person. That one person should be able to offer you everything. That they should bear that responsibility. That someone could offer everything to another person. Or that I myself could offer everything to one person. No one human being can give another human being everything. No, I have not allowed myself to lose control. I have not allowed myself to feel that. I do not want to be in a situation where I cannot imagine life without that one person. I would not want my husband to be unable to imagine life without me. That the loss would be too great to bear.

I appreciate that happiness isn't the only single correct emotion and that some feelings should be wrestled into submission. I am consciously grateful for all the good things there are in my life and there are indeed plenty. But I am beginning to understand that I will always have a hole in my soul. That possibly everyone has this feeling to a greater or lesser extent. A feeling of inadequacy. Of something vital missing from life. Sometimes the hole increases in size and at other times it decreases. But like most holes it can be repaired. And as it grows I try and fix it. I am learning how to mend this hole and hopefully I will be able to make the void smaller, but I am aware that it is always there.

There is so little that we really know about each other. I have so much more I want to share with you. I think to myself. I find it hard to visualise your life. I just can't imagine it. The one I am not a part of. The one I know so little about. Your other life. Our lives are so different. Our life experiences with varying degrees of similarities. I have always felt so close to you. Yet you are so far away.

Unlike the multi-coloured dahlias in my garden, some loves never bloom. Some loves never flourish. Some loves live under the ground. You have been buried away for so long.

"There are always flowers for those who want to see them."

– Henri Matisse

"A good head and a good heart are always a formidable combination."

– Nelson Mandela

MONDAY 20 JULY, 2014

My husband makes me laugh, but he doesn't always understand me. My husband likes to help people. He is very calm. Sometimes too calm. I am a bit of an enigma to him. Amongst other things my husband finds me cute, but not irresistible. I, amongst other things, find him strong and kind and on the whole very supportive of me. I appreciate what he does for me. I know we love each other very much. I wouldn't want to be without him. For the first six months of our marriage we enjoyed a long distance relationship. We married and lived apart until his work allowed him to relocate. After the first year of marriage I went to my mother and told her that this life was not for me. She said you have a good man. Remember it's only the face that changes. That was very sound advice and I live by it. And it's true. I like to see the part of him I fell in love with when we met. It makes me remember why I fell in love with him. My husband who challenges me and takes me out of my comfort zone. My husband who is so nonjudgmental. My husband who I had told and who accepts me for who I am. My husband who does not punish me or himself.

Over the years we have pushed each other apart. Somehow and so far we have thankfully managed to pull ourselves back together again. It is not always easy but we both work hard at our marriage. Often I think it is easier to leave a marriage than it is to stay and work through the difficult periods. When things are going well I don't want to think about things going badly. I knew the night I met my husband that I was going to marry him. I know that my husband was sent to me. By whom, I don't know. I knew that he would be able to challenge me. And I am right on that fact. He challenges me and we respect each other. He is as strong as I am, if not stronger in some ways. And he knows his own mind. He has his own ideas, which more often than not are different to mine. If my husband were to leave me it wouldn't be because of the wrinkles on my body or because of the lines on my face, it would be because of the venom that comes out of my mouth. I always knew at the end of each relationship what I didn't want in the next. I never knew what I wanted from marriage. My past relationships had taught me well. When I married my husband I knew what I didn't want. But I didn't know what I was going to get. My husband tells me: 'I always love you but I don't always like you.' He is right. I feel the same way about him.

I have often asked my husband the same question that I have repeatedly asked myself. We laugh and smile. But cannot find the answer to my question. *How did we end up together and how have we managed to make it work?* We are so different. To be completely honest I can say I wasn't ever particularly interested in marriage. I was never one of those girls who dreamt of the big day and the wedding dress. But I fell in love. Something I do not regret. I do see marriage as an anchor. My husband and I are very close. He is very patient with me. I live by my emotions. He is rational. My husband is intellectually curious. *Does he consider me his soul mate?* I don't believe in one soul mate per person. I would have met someone else if not him. But I am pleased I met him. I see that look in his eye. The one that tells me how much he loves me. He tells me all the time. I care endlessly. 'I care for you,' my husband tells me. And I know it's true. I do not actually believe in the one. But he is a real diamond. An almost flawless one. We have a lot of happiness. Many people say that marriage is an attraction of opposites, and in our case, this is definitely true. If life were just black and white it would be so much easier. But it isn't. We live in a world of compromise. Marriage and life itself are both full of compromises.

Because I have asked my husband so many questions over the years I have had to deal with answers I haven't always wanted to hear. He has always told me to ask the tough questions. I have learnt to be prepared for the answer whatever it may be. I have never seen my husband lose his temper. But he can go ice cold. He can be ruthless. But never with me. Was it his childhood that taught him to be so disconnected? My husband says people are basically an accumulation of their past experiences and memories. He is right. Men and women are so very different. But we know that. We laugh a lot together. I say real men aren't afraid of their feminine side. My husband reminds me this is not an original thought. But it is true. And he is afraid of his. My husband and I joke about why we chose each other. And indeed who chose who. My husband is a Sagittarius. A fire sign. Like me. I am an Aries. My older son is an Aries. My younger son is a Virgo. Like you.

My husband, the man who makes me feel so safe whether we are in the same room or on different continents. My husband travels a lot for work. My husband, who I am always happy to see when he comes home. My husband, who is still handsome. When we met he had dark brown hair and dark brown eyes. And when I looked into his eyes I could only see kindness then. Today my husband's hair is salt and pepper grey. The thin plait he used to have in 1986 long gone. The earring too. But when I look into his dark brown eyes today, I still see only kindness there. My husband, who says he can't fall asleep when I'm not there next to him. Neither when he is away. Nor when he is at home. I listen to his breathing as he sleeps. I was going to say laborious but it isn't. It is silent. He is relaxed. So rare. So nice to hear and watch. His peacefulness which he transfers to me. My husband, who is learning to understand my needs. My husband, who says he has no needs. Our relationship is more tender than passionate.

My glass is always half full. But my husband's sadly is always half empty. My husband doesn't always recognise, appreciate or utilise my capabilities. Sometimes I feel that I live my life in a gilded cage. After twenty-seven years of marriage I accept that my husband is cheered up by what I can't do. And I seriously don't mind at all. I am learning that I have a voice. And I am allowed to be heard. And I am listened to when I speak. My husband is my linchpin. My support system. He helps me to hold together the various elements of my rather complicated structure. My husband is one of the most able people I know. He keeps me anchored and I in turn add life to his existence. He takes good care of me. My husband says he manages very well without me, but even better with me.

My husband says you only learn when you start realising how little you really know. When I am told I can't or won't be able to do something, I retreat. No one should ever tell me I can't do something because it takes my insides out and makes me not want to even try. At times inside there is a steel wall and I am impenetrable. It can come down without a warning. When I go it's like I want to leave. But I always come back. When the hood comes down, I feel a sense of panic. Not wanting to be there. I just go away, to be by myself. Then I come back. I always come back.

The past is another life. Today the most radical thing one can do is get married and live a conventional life. Most people celebrate their birthdays automatically. Everybody has the right to celebrate their birthday. But we earn the right to celebrate a wedding anniversary. Next year when I am fifty-six years old, I will have been married for exactly half my life. That feels huge. And you. You have already been married for over half of your life. *How does that feel for you?*

"Marriage can be a magnificent lesson in becoming our best selves; that is true."
– Marianne Williamson

"An invisible red thread connects those who are destined to meet, regardless of time, place or circumstance. The thread may stretch or tangle, but it will never break."

– Chinese Proverb

MARCH 1994

Between the years of 1989 and 1994 both of us had moved to new homes with our respective families. We had kept each other updated with our new addresses and telephone numbers, always managing to keep that thread of contact going. Still, neither of us wanting to let go completely. Always making sure that the one knew where the other was. I received your postcard in 1994. I still have it, amongst my treasures. In big bold letters at the top you had written: 'Urgent. Please forward'. I have definitely told you the story of how it eventually found its way into my hands. *But do you remember?* Probably not. You had sent a postcard to my old address, from where we had moved about six months previously. During the extremely long but not particularly hot school summer holidays. At the end of the academic year of nursery school. And before the start of primary school. That transitional period.

The new owner of our old house had phoned to say that a postcard had arrived for me and that it should be collected, at my earliest possible convenience. Seeing as we hadn't moved too far away I went almost as soon as I had put the phone down from her. In other words, immediately. I was intrigued. I remember wondering whilst on my way what could be written on this postcard and who was it from. What was the importance and significance of it? What was the sense of urgency I had detected in this woman's voice? This woman, whom I had only ever met once before. This woman, who clearly felt a very strong need to get this postcard to me. Many would have just ignored it and thrown it in the bin.

As she placed the postcard in my hand, I knew it was from you. Your distinctive handwriting immediately recognisable with your very original signature. That feeling. Always. The pounding heart. I remember the look in her eye as she handed the postcard to me. It was somewhat quizzical. As if she knew. Any news from you was good news. And when I read it I realised this postcard stated the best news imaginable. I could not have thanked her any more than I did for the kindness, sensitivity and understanding she had shown me by ensuring that the postcard arrived to its rightful owner. Me.

HEY GIRLIE,
CALL ME. CAN'T FIND YOUR NUMBER. GOING TO A CONVENTION IN FRANCE AND HAVE DECIDED TO TAKE A CHANCE AND COME BACK TO LONDON AND PAY YOU A VISIT. HOW DOES THAT SOUND? ARRIVING ON APRIL 8TH. IT'S ONLY BEEN TEN YEARS!

LOVE ALWAYS
XX

I can remember the immediate feeling of excitement I felt after having read your postcard. You were due to arrive in a couple of weeks. It was unbelievable. Even to me; in fact, it was totally incomprehensible. After all this time you were coming back to London. You hadn't been able to get hold of me on the phone. Unsurprisingly, we were ex-directory. This was before the days of mobiles. Well for us at least. Back then mobiles were a rarity and an extravagance. I had no need for one. I do remember the requisite list of names and companies to whom I had notified of our forthcoming move. You know there are the people who you have to notify and the ones you want to notify. And the ones you don't tell because you don't want them in your life anymore. I know that you were on the want to notify list. This was before either of us had access to email.

It transpired I had let you know but that you had hidden away my new details. So deeply hidden away was this piece of information that you couldn't find it when you had wanted it and needed it. I would never have left you off any list of mine. The new owner had indeed read the postcard. She had sensed your urgency and taken it seriously. Well you had told her in any event. I was given the postcard two weeks before your arrival. How very clever of you to write a postcard. How very typical of you to hide something away so safely that you wouldn't be able to find it. *Were you coming specifically to see me?* I don't know. I shall ask you.

There had been relatively little contact between us since 1989. We had more or less completely lost contact soon after I had had my first child. Or at least I couldn't remember any significant contact. Although I do remember quite vividly speaking to you on the day that I came home from hospital with my firstborn son. You had called me on that day. Out of the blue. It was almost like you knew. There had been the occasional birthday card. The occasional Christmas card and the even more occasional phone call. By the time I had received your postcard in 1994 telling me of your imminent arrival I had two children. My second son was born in 1991. The years had passed. I was now a full-time mother. With one child about to leave nursery and the other about to start. I had taken up painting and loved it. A friend and I had set up and were running an art gallery in the local garden centre. I was enjoying both the painting and the running of the gallery, which was only open on the weekends. Otherwise by appointment. On one of the days on the weekend my husband would look after the children, which would enable me to man the gallery. It was a situation that worked well. My husband enjoyed his time alone with the children and I enjoyed interacting with the people who came to the gallery. I knew that you were now a photographer, although I had seen very little of your work. You had turned your hobby into your career.

The years were passing and times were busy for both of us. There was barely time to breathe. Let alone think. About anything or anyone outside of my everyday life. But whenever I thought of you I did so with such deep affection. Not that I thought of you everyday. Don't be absurd. But at times more than others. Always fondly. I hadn't wanted to think about you too often during the last ten years since you had returned home. But whenever I did it was always with a smile on my face. Fate again intervened when the new owner of our old house called me, to tell me about the postcard that was waiting for me there. We were destined not to lose touch. I had buried you away. Along with my father. You were from my other life. The life I had led before I had married.

"If you love somebody, let them go, for if they return, they were always yours. And if they don't, they never were."

– Kahlil Gibran

"Start with what is right rather than what is acceptable."
– Franz Kafka

THURSDAY 30 JULY, 2014

Over the years there has been the occasional opportunity of forsaking my marriage vows and throwing away the monogamy title, but somehow I have never felt the need or desire. I have not wanted to. But with you it is different. You were mine first. You were always mine. Why does monogamy seem to represent such a challenge? Because although we like the idea, the reality of being part of a couple, faithful for ever, actually seeing it through is another thing. Committing yourself to one person is hard and it only seems to be getting harder. I wonder whether nature intended us to be monogamous. *Do you think we're supposed to be?* I'm not sure that we are. Otherwise it wouldn't be so difficult, would it? What is better? To embark on a damaging affair or go through life with the nagging suspicion that we could be having more.

I view my sexuality as an integral part of my body and my being. If it were to be taken from me, I would feel as if a body part had been taken from me. Things aren't always forgotten. They are lost. Events in my life have had an impact on my body. I like to think that I know my body well and that my body knows me well. I like to dance. It is liberating. If my body's not fit, then I feel my mind is out of shape too.

I am not sure that we are an animal created to be happy. I think that we are created to reproduce. The happiness we find is the happiness we make ourselves. And I think that we can make good relationships with other people. I think that every relationship is different. Attraction is varied and complex. I believe people get together and stay together for a multitude of reasons.

I ask myself: *What do I want? And how do I get it?* There's something about someone who knows and understands you well. It never goes. I have this burning desire to talk to you. To touch you. To feel you in real time. Not just in my heart. I allow you to get into my head and that's a place I don't let anyone go. I don't even go there myself. Is this too much to ask? Isn't this what friendships are all about? *What kind of friendship do we have?*

I like to think about the changes that have taken place in both my life and during my lifetime. I like to think about what is totally acceptable now. How poignant and powerful some of these changes have been. Changes in attitudes, health, standards of living. Acceptance of homosexuality. Acceptance of mixed marriages. How have these changes affected me? I think about my family and where they came from. What have I learned from the previous generations?

Now I see how times have changed. But that was then and this is now.

Irrespective of anyone's gender. Neither gender nor sexuality is important to me. But the person is. And this is the principle on which my relationships have always been based. It seems to me that people get defined by their relationships. I don't like being defined by my relationships.

It seems to me that we form different relationships with different people. I do not believe one person can give you everything. Different needs in us are fuelled by different people. How I relate to one particular person will be a totally different experience as to how another person relates to that same person.

"Times and conditions change so rapidly that we must keep our aim constantly focused on the future."
– Walt Disney

"Happiness often sneaks in through a door you didn't know you left open."

– John Barrymore

APRIL 1994

I remember how I had anticipated your visit. I remember the excitement. I remember the emotions the thought of your arrival evoked in me. The most overwhelming emotion being of pure pleasure at the opportunity of being able to spend time together. Finally, you are coming to visit and I needed to think about the changes and developments that had occurred and which I had experienced during the ten-year period since we had last seen each other. I certainly didn't have much time to think. Your arrival I remember was almost imminent. But of course you could come and stay. You would always be welcome in my home. Wherever my home was and whenever you wanted to visit. I would always welcome you with open arms and an open heart. My life had changed dramatically. The years had passed since I had met you in 1984. My life was so different now. As was yours. I was now married with two children. As were you. I was leading a different life. But I was still me. Or at least I think and hoped I was. *Would you still be you?*

The interim years between 1984 and 1994 had been busy, different, life changing. I knew they had been for you too. Nappies and nurseries. I was also now painting and running a gallery that I had set up with a friend. A place where other artists could also sell their paintings, in the local garden centre. You were now a photographer. Of fashion, food and cars. As you said later we had been getting on with our own lives during the last ten years. Finally, you were returning to London. Albeit for only one night. I hadn't seen you for ten years. Literally. Not even a photo. I had barely even spoken to you. Contact had been extremely limited. Phone calls had been so expensive. I remember that. Communication had been hard to control. I didn't have access to the internet yet. The time difference was awkward. And our friendship. Yes our friendship. I couldn't define or explain that one. But you were always there. Hidden away in that special place in my heart. Reserved solely for you. Your secret place in my heart.

My memories are so terribly vague but you did come and stay. I don't remember how we made the arrangement. It must have been on the phone. Clearly in my excitement I had confused the time of your arrival. You pitched up really early on the arranged day. I hadn't even had my shower and I opened the door not expecting to see you. I was gutted. I had the whole dressing gown and pillow hair thing going on. Foggy head too. And two children hanging around my ankles. I thought it was going to be the postman. So did the kids. I remember being really flustered. You seem to be able to evoke that emotion in me quite easily.

I remember how much I had been looking forward to seeing you after ten years. I was leading a very different life now. But so were you. Perhaps I had become a different person too. Maybe you had changed also. But I needn't have worried. As soon as I saw you I knew that we both still felt the same way. I saw it in your eyes and felt it in my heart. A deep recognition. You looked almost exactly the same. Just older, wiser, bruised and slightly battered. But still the same you. I had told my husband about you many years ago. Right at the beginning of our relationship. Not long after my husband and I had met at a mutual friend's wedding. I'm not sure why I told him. Probably because I knew he wouldn't judge me. I had wanted him to know how important you were to me. Because I hadn't felt the need to hide to you. I wasn't the one who had been engaged to someone else during our time together. I had been single at the time.

Over the years and on the odd occasion I have spoken about you to my husband. But he has never had the opportunity of meeting you. Now he will. Because you were coming to stay. For one night. I was going to see you for the first time in ten years. Since we have been married my husband has often said to me: 'Have no expectations and you will not be disappointed.' I have no expectations from you. I also know that you will never disappoint me. I know so little about your everyday life. But I know you. And I am sure not just from this life either.

You were as funny, as witty and as charming as I had remembered. And still as attractive too. You looked as lovely as I had remembered. The same as the image I had held in my memory for all those years. And when I touched you, I cannot believe I felt that same connection immediately. It was a very strange sensation. I don't want to let go of you. That feeling. Still there. When I am next to you. By your side. After all these years. How could there have been such a connection after ten years of not having seen you. I knew you felt the same way. There was so much to tell you. So much to catch up with. And I really didn't know where to start.

We took my kids to the park and played on the swings. One was nearly five and the other almost three years old. Practically the same ages as your two children. Both of our respective elder children had been born within a month of each other. It had been the same with our younger two. Your two children were a month older than both of mine. I was now thirty-five and you were thirty-three. We watched the children whilst they played in the sandpit. And when the kids had tired of the sandpit we played hide and seek the four of us. We hid and the children sought us out. We stole a hidden kiss. Of course, I haven't forgotten. Perhaps that was a little irresponsible; however, it didn't feel so at the time.

When we got back home you baked us your delicious banana bread, which for years afterwards, and even to this day, I still make. I remember how you mashed up the bananas and let the children lick the bowl. I miss the smell of baking in the home now that the children have gone and I am often alone. In my quiet times I like to bake. And whilst I bake I think of you. Full of sweetness. Like the shortbread I have just made. Yes I remember. I do have something that belongs to you. I have your recipes. And every time I bake your banana bread and take it out of the oven, I make a conscious effort not to burn my fingers like you did. It makes me smile. Such a perfectionist. I always thought it was such a lovely gesture to bake. All the happiness and love that went in with the ingredients to make the banana bread. Your special recipe, which in turn funnily enough has become one of my signature dishes. I know why I adore you. I remember.

My husband travels a lot for work. And at relatively short notice. And for short amounts of time. He is always home for the weekend. The children are almost too young to notice his absence during the week. They are often asleep by the time he comes home from the office. We both enjoy our space. Our time apart. We both enjoy our reunions. Our time together. I am always pleased when he comes home. He is still handsome. His plait and earring both long gone. My husband was away for work the night you came to stay. I can't remember where he went. You never met.

I had wanted to give you a taste of my life during your very short visit. We had gone to the park. We had stolen a hidden kiss. We had hidden a stolen kiss. We had talked. We had baked. We had laughed. We had even cried. Both of us. Tears of laughter. And tears of sadness. But many more tears of laughter. In the evening Alex came round. Alex who had spent the day dressing a set for a music video. Alex was an assistant art director designing sets and supervising their building and dressing. Alex who was loving life. Alex who was working hard. And gaining recognition. And a good working reputation. Alex who was playing even harder. Alex who was not married. You and Alex were so pleased to see each other.

The three of us went for a meal at Casa Mia. One of my favourite local restaurants. It reminded me of The Soho Café in many ways. The Soho Café where we had met ten years earlier in 1984. Casa Mia was a small, intimate café style Italian restaurant hidden away in a largely residential side-street. It was easy to miss and I had discovered it only by using the road as a cut-through. The premises were nothing to look at. A double-fronted shop front that could well have been a delicatessen. It was almost like a conversion of the front room of a house. A tiny little Italian restaurant full of loud staff and tables too close together. Casa Mia is a café during the day and turns into a restaurant in the evening. It is rather cramped but worth it for the fabulous food we enjoyed. Good quality authentic Italian cuisine served by authentic Italian staff in a friendly and hospitable atmosphere. The service was efficient and unobtrusive. The three of us had a wonderful time that evening. Alex was so happy to see you. You were thrilled to see Alex. I was delighted to be with you both. Just the three of us. In our own world. Alex listened as we spoke about our children. Another world completely. That was strange. To talk about our children. You and me. Something I would never have anticipated talking about all those years ago when we met in 1984. We laughed. As we always had. It seemed that you and I had even more to talk about now. Not that I can remember what we used to talk about then. It was like going back in time. As if the last ten years had been wiped away. Just for that evening. The feeling. Still there. For both of us.

The next morning, I remember the lingering kiss in the car when I dropped you at the tube station. I was concerned we would be spotted. You agreed. We felt each other's pain. I can remember watching you walk towards the platform into the distance. As quickly as you had reappeared you had disappeared. As suddenly as you had come back into my life. You had left again. But you never really left. It's uncertain when we'll meet again but I know I'll catch you on the flip side.

You told me that you had taken a chance by coming

to London. Sometimes in life you only get one chance and that one chance may never be repeated. I really don't remember much about your actual visit. But I remember certain events. That you arrived on the day Kurt Cobain was found dead in his home. Apparently of a single self-inflicted gunshot wound. It had upset us both. But particularly you. Being a Nirvana fan. My memories are particularly vague of that time we shared together. I'm not sure why. Although of course I do have some memories. I remember your arrival. I remember your departure. I certainly remember our goodbye. I remember our hello too. I remember our stolen kiss in the park. How could I forget that. The rest is a bit of a blank. Like an artist's unpainted canvas.

"Beware of missing chances, otherwise it may be altogether too late some day."

– Franz Liszt

"Letters had always defeated distance, but with the coming of e-mail, time seemed to be vanquished as well."

– Thomas Mallon

FRIDAY 29 AUGUST, 2014

Since receiving your email in June telling me of your forthcoming arrival at the beginning of September, I have taken this opportunity to reflect over our emails from 2007 to the present day. Knowing that you would be here soon I had retrieved them from my hidden folder, which I thought I had deleted. Apparently not all of them. It's strange. I have found emails I didn't even know existed. Firstly, I thought I had deleted all emails from you. Secondly, when I found they hadn't all been deleted, it was like reading some of them for the very first time. I have been reading them over the last few weeks. Remembering and reminiscing.

Nearly every one of these emails mentions how you are trying to engineer a visit. But these occasions never manifested themselves. You wanted to. I knew that. But you hadn't succeeded. You had been hoping to surprise me in early 2008. You had been booked on a three-week job in Paris only to see it go to a different company to the one that had held you. That would have been great, but it never materialised. In 2010 you had mentioned the possibility of a seminar in Amsterdam and that you hoped you would be able to come over at the end to say hi. That you wanted to tag me onto the end of a business trip, but that you rarely travelled to Europe for work. I knew that anyway. And in 2011 you had mentioned the possibility of coming to London after a family holiday in Italy. Alone. That obviously wasn't going to happen. I remember you telling me how sick you were on that particular trip. You had also written to say that you were going to try and come over for the Olympics. But the 2012 London Olympics came and went. And again you were a no show.

I don't know why I hadn't wanted to Skype when you first asked me to in 2008. Perhaps it was for the best. Your emails are so beautiful but I realise that I know so little about you; in fact, we know so little about each other. But always that feeling. Before emails there were occasional texts and phone calls and of course that postcard. The one telling me of your imminent arrival back in 1994. The postcard the new owner of our old house had made sure that I received. But suddenly we seem to find the time to email and WhatsApp. In anticipation of your visit. Backwards and forwards over the seas. No Skyping. I hadn't wanted to. I am not sure why. Fear of the actual Skyping process or was it the fear that I may disappoint you. Who knows? I do. The former not the latter. We conduct our friendship in secret because we want to.

We had started to email and WhatsApp in anticipation of your visit. Fortunately, both of us being able to tell the other different memories from our short-lived past together. Both of us happy to share our own separate memories. Remembering and reminding each other of the times that we had shared together. Different memories but the same feeling for both of us. And then we started to learn new things about each other. We started to learn about each other. Nothing to do with the past but about who we had become. Both of us realising and enjoying how easy it was to rebuild our old friendship. Particularly with such strong foundations that were built all those years ago in 1984. We understood each other. I began to recognise your moods from your emails. We spoke a couple of times. But mostly we communicated by email or WhatsApp. We wrote until we were due to meet. I didn't tell you.

My memories of your visit and that one night we spent together in 1994 are so faded. Over the years I have been preoccupied with the strong memories that I still have of what occurred sometime after you had left. I know some of the things that happened to you. You know the things I have chosen to tell you about myself. But this I never told you. I want to tell you now. Now is better than never. Maybe I should have said something before. I could never have envisaged the profound and long lasting effect your visit would have on me. But you are from my other life.

I want to tell you what happened some months after your visit in 1994, because suddenly you are coming to London. Predominantly to visit your son, but also to see me. The first time we will have seen each other since 1994. When you came to stay. When we took my children to the park and played hide and seek. And stole a hidden kiss. And hid a stolen kiss. That feeling still there. For both of us. When we went out for supper—you, me and Alex—I was so excited to see you. To hold you. But I am also concerned as I think you ought to know. And please understand why I haven't told you before now. I'm not sure why I feel the need to tell you now. *Is it because you are coming to the UK?* I don't want to hurt you. Sometimes I am too honest. I have been told I have no filter. I don't want to hurt anyone. Ever. That is not my intention. It never has been. And it never will be. Particularly not you. Never. I am in two minds as to whether I should tell you or not.

For so many years I was preoccupied with the chain of events that arose after your departure. Starting with that phone call. My memories of your visit almost erased. But not those awful feelings of emptiness, loneliness and disbelief. That you had come back into my life. And that you had left it again. Those feelings have not been erased. The memories of what happened afterwards forever ingrained in my memory bank. The memories that won't and don't go away. The really horrible ones. It doesn't matter to me that I have forgotten so much about your visit. I have not forgotten the feeling of being with you and I never will.

I remember the lovely phone calls. We used to speak for ages. For a period of weeks. Months even. You tell me that you don't remember those conversations. The ones we had after your visit. The ones that meant so much to me. The ones that gave me so much pleasure. But that's OK. You have other beautiful memories that escape me. What are your memories of that visit I wonder? After you returned home I know what you were up to. You told me. I know what I call those days of yours. So do you. I did not run into another's arms. But I understood. You had wanted to matter to someone again. Someone who was near to you physically. And it couldn't be me. I was nearly 5,500 miles away. I never told you what I went through. I want to share this with you now.

And then of course contact ceased between us. Our friendship once again disrupted. For a very long time. I'm sure you remember why. I do. We had no choice. We had to keep away from each other. That was hard. So very hard. After having had such regular contact for so many months since your visit. But again I understood. As always. Our friendship once again restricted. I knew the rules. I just didn't like them. But I could play the game perfectly. I will play by your rules. Even when they are changed. I have no choice if I want to play at all. We both played by the rules. Always. Although I am not so sure if that is true. Why hadn't you felt my need all those years ago? Was it because you were dealing with the torrent of abuse that was being hurled in your direction at the very same time? Always parallel lives. Different experiences. The same feeling. Always.

And when we reconnected sometime later after an understandably long period of radio silence, I never told you. I couldn't tell you. Not on the phone at any rate. But now that you are coming I do want to tell you. I am not sure why I want you to know. I am unsure of my reasons for wanting to tell you. And if there is really any point. I am not a bad person. But you already know that to your detriment. Over the last two decades I can only remember having spoken openly about what happened on two occasions. But not to you. I have chosen to bury this experience and my memories of that occasion. But there will always be the occasional moment when memories come flooding back. Had it not been for your imminent arrival, I feel sure these memories would have remained locked away forever.

Is it possible to get someone from your past to be part of your present? Yes. It's very simple to move beyond memories and sentiment and start almost completely afresh. Not having to rely on the memories from our youth. Not needing to overlook whether or not we are compatible in the future. Just knowing. The person who I adore. I always have and fear I always will. It's exciting engaging in such a friendship. You chose me. Nothing is by chance. Do you think we were together in another life? Don't you find it strange that we even met? Did I let you slip away or did you let me go? There is so much to tell you and I really don't know where to start.

Us the romantics. The pair with the half-full glasses or in my case the three-quarters full one. It's bizarre. It's strange. How much you can begin to learn about someone from emails and WhatsApps. The power of silence. Although I miss the sound of your voice. I am learning your likes and dislikes.

Despite having spent thirty years apart, and not having seen you for twenty years other than the occasional photograph, the bond between us is unbroken. And I know I want to tell you and indeed you have asked me what has been going on at my end. I have realised I have nothing that belongs to you. No transitional object. Once you sent me a photo of your beautiful dog. Funny how they say that dogs look like their owners and vice versa. The same soulful eyes. Beautiful dog. Beautiful you.

It's so strange, I have nothing that belongs to you. Maybe your heart. But nothing that you have given to me. There is nothing tangible I can look at and say: 'Oh, this is from you.' Or, 'That belonged to you.' I only have six photos of you over a thirty-year period. In each of the photos you are laughing. I love your laugh. I love your smile. When I look at the photos I can hear your laughter. How can it be that I don't have one photograph of us together? Not only that but I have probably seen only five or six different photos of you over the last twenty years. Your image so clear in my head. Unchanged over the years. You are vain but modest too. I like the way you look after and take care of yourself. I cannot believe I am the only person who has ever told you that you are vain. Perhaps you have only ever revealed your true self to me.

"A woman has to live her life, or live to repent not having lived it."

– D.H. Lawrence

"We are made wise, not by the recollection of our past, but by the responsibility for our future."
– George Bernard Shaw

MONDAY 1 SEPTEMBER, 2014

Sensitive, gentle and thoughtful soul. I want and need to know more about you and I want to tell you more about myself. I haven't wanted to tell you anything that might put a blot on the excitement of your first visit in twenty years. I haven't told you what happened after your last visit. But I will. When we meet. I haven't told you where I had been in 2004. I want to tell you all these things now when we meet. Tomorrow. I also want to tell you my reasons for not having told you before now. But I'm not so sure I know what these reasons are any longer. I have so much to tell you. So much has happened in my life. And there is so much I want to hear about you and your life. *I have so much more I want to share with you*, I think to myself.

My feelings for you have grown more intense over the last few weeks, as you have begun to hover on the edge of my day-to-day life. You have become more real to me. The advancement and development of communication has benefited us no end. *Or has it?* You have entered my life. But you are from my other life. The elation I feel when I hear from you. The disappointment when I don't. You are my drug. Not my raison d'être. Now is better than never and maybe

I should have said something before. I don't know why but suddenly I am overwhelmed with the idea that now is the time to tell you what I should have told you some twenty years ago. I am your secret. Perhaps it was time to tell you one of mine. Now was as good a time as ever. To tell you. To tell you the truth. To tell you what happened. To apologise. I don't know. I must be careful. What the outcome would be I didn't know. But I had to tell you. Well, the truth is I wanted you to know. Because of your imminent arrival. The thought of looking you in the eye and not telling you after all these years was an impossibility. You would see it on my face before the words came out. I knew that you would still have the ability to read me like a book.

You read about people like us all the time. They all have their own reasons for why they can't be together. *What were our reasons then?* I can remember. *What are our reasons now?* I can't answer that one. Always so many questions. And so few answers. We are surely not isolated in our situation?

Sleep doesn't come easily to me and there have been a few long dark nights over the last couple of months, but then there is plenty of time to sleep when I get to the other side. I can't believe that tomorrow we will meet. After twenty years. The last time I saw you was when I dropped you off at East Finchley tube station in 1994. After you had come to stay for one night. You had taken a chance by coming to London on your way back from a convention in France. The last time I had seen you we had shared a lingering kiss. In my car. On the forecourt of my local tube station. I had been nervous that we would be seen. That our kiss would be spotted. I was not nervous that we would be seen at Shepherd's Bush tube station. Where we are meeting tomorrow. I cannot wait. I am beyond excited.

"Though sleep is called our best friend, it is a friend who often keeps us waiting!"
— Jules Verne

"I believe that we are solely responsible for our choices, and we have to accept the consequences of every deed, word, and thought throughout our lifetime."

– Elisabeth Kubler-Ross

TUESDAY 2 SEPTEMBER, 2014

I should have realised that you would get to the station early and that you would be waiting for me. Your advantage. Without a doubt. Well played. It didn't cross my mind to get there before the prearranged time of 9.30am. I never thought. Silly me. With hindsight I would so much have loved to have seen you come out of the station.

From before I had even caught sight of you. From before I had exited from the station I knew how our liaison would continue. As I was walking towards the daylight, the exit turnstiles and you. I had stepped off the escalator and as I was approaching the exit I received what I can only assume was a warning. I barely had time to register but I knew as I felt that punch in my stomach. The one that had literally stopped me in my stride. That feeling of being winded. A warning like I have never had before. Who was it from? And what was I being warned against? I didn't know.

Immediately, I had spotted you sitting on the bench. Basking in the early morning sunshine. As attractive as you had always been. And as you tilted your head ever so slightly towards my direction our eyes had locked. Your smile. That look. Especially for me. The Oyster card I had topped up the previous day in preparation wouldn't allow me out of the turnstile. Was this another warning? It wouldn't connect. I was trying to 'touch out' the Oyster card on the yellow card reader at the turnstile in absolute desperation. But to no avail. The only thought going through my head at that particular moment being *please let me out!* Still winded from the imaginary punch I had received. I was overwhelmed. I laughed that I couldn't get to you. Nervous laughter. I panicked. I could barely look at you. Your smile had turned into laughter. Still that sensation. As always.

I ran looking for assistance. For someone to let me out. I felt so foolish. Eventually after what seemed like hours—but was probably only a matter of seconds—a guard came to my aid. He 'touched out' my Oyster card for me. Miraculously the turnstile opened and I was able to get out of the station. There had been absolutely no problem with my card. You told me later that I was still the same and you had watched my panic with amusement. You must have enjoyed that. Meanwhile, I had broken out into a sweat. I cannot believe that I couldn't get out of the station. This was our reunion after twenty years.

After all the hype, the excitement, the wanting and the anticipation, the reality of our reunion played out very differently to my fantasy. In my mind I had imagined that we would bump into each other on the tube. I had had this ridiculous idea that we would see each other across a crowded carriage. And that we wouldn't be able to get to each other until the tube had stopped. But it didn't happen like that at all. I have replayed the moment of our reunion in my mind. So many times. Over and over again. And each time I remember something else or feel differently. Differently but overall and always the same feeling. I am not sure what to call this feeling. It is impossible to put into words. For me there is no name. There is no label. In fact, it seems to me that our reunions have never gone to plan. But then again does anything in life ever go to plan? Remembering back to the one in 1994. When you arrived very early on the arranged day at my home. And caught me unawares. I had opened the front door not yet showered and with pillow hair. Not expecting you until a couple of hours later. I had thought it was going to be the postman. I had two children hanging around my ankles. They had thought it was going to be the postman too. I remember feeling very flustered. An emotion you still seem to be able to evoke in me today.

Initially I had wanted to go to an exhibition with you. This was what I had really wanted to do. Once you had told me that you were coming to London. This was my dream. To walk around an exhibition with you. And I had known immediately which one I had wanted to take you to. But this particular exhibition had rather sadly ended a couple of days before your arrival. The exhibition, like yourself, was on its way to another part of the world. Maybe even your part. I don't know. I had put Plan B into action. I smile to myself as I write this. I am well known for always having a Plan B.

We had arranged to meet outside Shepherd's Bush tube station. From here we would make our way together to The Hummingbird Café. I seem to associate you and cafés together. It's understandable really when I think back to our chance meeting. We had met thirty years earlier in May 1984. Whilst we had both been working at a café. The Soho Café. But we had been working on opposite shifts. Although we discovered later that we had both started in the same week. A month prior to our meeting. I can remember the day that we found each other. The day that we met. The day that changed our lives. I had swapped a shift with Charlie. As a good turn. As a favour for Charlie. That was the day we met by chance.

I had chosen The Hummingbird Café from its excellent reviews on TripAdvisor. For it's full bodied flat white coffee. The drink I now preferred compared to the cappuccinos I used to enjoy thirty years ago. I had seen a photo too on TripAdvisor of the delicious vegetarian breakfast. Which would suit you. Now that you were a vegetarian. I had done my research. As always. I had also chosen The Hummingbird Café because of its proximity to where we were meeting.

Apparently the café was equidistant between the tube station and your hotel. Very close by. It seemed to suit our needs. Both of ours. The ideal place to go to after not having seen someone for twenty years. The perfect place for a lingering brunch. Where we could decide together what to do for the rest of the day. The Hummingbird Café was a small, independent, antipodean style café in the heart of Shepherd's Bush that was hidden away down a side street. We could sit outside and would be able to enjoy the sights and sounds in the street as we attempted to catch up on the last two decades. I had read on the reviews that some people had found this café by mistake. We couldn't find it at all. Not even by using the map. We had stood side-by-side laughing and looking at the enlarged street map of the area that was on the wall at the exit of the tube station. We had tried to get to the café and couldn't find it. Neither of us being able to identify the route to take from the map. Both of us totally confused and totally unfocused. How were we going to get ourselves there? My sense of direction is appalling at the best of times. One of my worst characteristics. I am always heading the wrong way. And at this precise moment it had totally disappeared.

Fully prepared for this possible eventuality, I had brought the phone number of the café with me written down on a scrap of paper. I phoned whilst we were standing at the station. Having given up on understanding the street map. Nerves overtook and between the two of us we couldn't follow the girl's instructions giving us directions to the café. We were standing at the tube station. Both of us powerless. I was definitely in a state of panic. I can't speak for you. I don't know what you were feeling. Probably the same. It was the most absurd situation. We couldn't stop laughing. I don't remember who made the suggestion. *Was it you or was it me?* But suddenly we were on the way to your hotel. Our attempt at finding the café lost forever.

You were staying at the rather hip K West Hotel in Shepherd's Bush of all places. It was a hyper-modern striking glass-cube and concrete boutique hotel. An edgy urban retreat where Victorian mansion blocks and terraced villas lined the rest of the small street. Near to Shepherd's Bush tube station and the Westfield shopping mall. The hotel's contemporary vibe attracted those from the music and media industries who enjoyed the proximity to the nearby Shepherd's Bush Empire and the Apollo. The hotel's energy attracting cool, relaxed and trendy individuals. I understood why you were staying here. But what was I doing in your room?

If walls could talk the rooms at K West would have a few stories to tell. As former BBC offices and recording studios, the guest rooms had soaked up the rock'n'roll essence of hallowed legends, such as Bob Marley and The Kinks. The perfect choice for you. The guitar playing you.

I was stunned at just how large the room was. It had a luxurious oversized bed. The room was decorated in a calming colour scheme of soft taupe, creams and browns. It was decked out with up-to-date gadgetry. Modern touches included an LCD flat screen TV, sandblasted glass, and original artwork which gave the room a distinctive stamp. The spacious bathroom had designer toiletries. The bank of grass was hidden from view by a great expanse of curtaining, which I opened immediately. I opened the window too. The warm sunny air filtered into the room. The view was strange.

As I had drawn back the curtains and flung open the window the first thing I saw ambling along the large grassy bank was an urban fox eyeballing me from about six feet away. In this very secluded and enclosed space. Never had a warning been clearer to me. The fox. A messenger. A sign of danger. A sign to be mindful of our surroundings. That much I did know. I seemed to be endlessly surrounded by foxes. The fox who beckons us to not make too many waves but rather adapt to our surroundings, blend into it, and use our surroundings and circumstances to our advantage. I often saw them at home. But here and so close and now. *Why?* I didn't know until later that the fox also symbolises passion, desire, intensity and expression. But I didn't express myself clearly that day. All the other emotions were there in that room with us. I understood the fox was there for a reason. I hadn't worked the reason out just yet. Just the interpretation. I was aware of the interpretation.

Immediately you made us both coffee. Proclaiming your disdain for the instant coffee that was all set up on a tray. I laughed. You taught me a new word. Barista. And as you sat down you immediately took off your socks and shoes. Still only wearing odd socks. Never a pair. After all these years. Old habits and superstitions die hard. I loved the way you did that. We laughed. As always.

I told you. Before I had even sat down in your lovely room, I told you what maybe I should have told you ten years ago. I could not wait until I had even sat down. What was so important that I had to tell you so quickly? This secret I had kept from you and so wanted to tell you. Or perhaps one of a number of secrets that I had wanted to tell you. There really are quite a few.

I felt your desire in that room. And you felt mine. You said *let's have a shower. Wash away the years.* But we didn't. You lay down on the bed first. I followed your lead. Fully clothed. We lay there together. Entwined. As if we had never been apart. It made me think how strange it was to hold you after so many years. How in my head I knew every inch of your body, but in truth it felt unfamiliar. Not what I was used to. But what I had yearned for and still do. You made me feel as if I had a warm cloak around me. This feeling is something that I didn't know I was missing and now I don't want to let it go. You got up first from the bed. I could read your mind. You had wanted to protect me from the multitude of suffering that you had endured over the years. Those feelings amongst others of pain, deceit and guilt.

I am going home on the tube and I am disappointed in myself for having said so much that maybe I shouldn't have said. And maybe I should have told you things that I didn't tell you. I am unsettled. I exposed myself. Almost completely. I am often told that I talk too much and don't listen enough. Something that my family tells me time and time again. That I should listen more and speak less. To interrupt less. Which I often do. It's probably my worst characteristic. But I seem to always have so many questions when people are telling their story. My family joke that I could never have become a prison officer because I can never let anyone finish a sentence. I think it's true. Sometimes I feel that my life is my own internal prison.

I told you some of my biggest secrets and a lot of my innermost feelings and fears. I feel a little disloyal to my family for having told you some of our deepest and darkest secrets. But it all just came tumbling out. You are emotionally curious. Our friendship is very comforting. I have told you so much about myself and my family, but you in turn have done the same. I am shocked by some of the things that you have shared with me. Why did I open up my heart to you after not having seen you for twenty years? I couldn't help myself. To be honest. It felt so natural. Like talking to a really old friend. As if we had picked up from where we had left off. I know you felt the same way. Just the subject matter had changed. Not the feeling. For either of us. How could I have let you slip away again like this? Never before have I ever wanted anyone like I want you.

"Distance does not break off the friendship absolutely, but only the activity of it."
— Aristotle

"Learn from yesterday, live for today, hope for tomorrow. The important thing is not to stop questioning."

– Albert Einstein

WEDNESDAY 3 SEPTEMBER, 2014

Last night in my dreams I found you and I kissed you. You kissed me back. With vehement passion. Always there. Even in my dreams. But this is the first dream that I have ever had of you. I hope it's a reoccurring one. I don't know where we were. But then of course it was only a dream. And then I had that nightmare again. Unfortunately, the one that does recur. Time and time again. It manifests itself in different ways. Surely this is not the way my subconscious wants me to behave. This is not me. Today I have woken feeling full of repentance for my actions in the nightmare. Thank goodness it wasn't real.

I want to trace the lines on your face. The lines that were never there before, but that have appeared over the years. Probably helped by the sun along with the torrent of abuse that has been thrown in your direction over so many years. You are battered but not totally beaten. You are worn but not dishevelled. You are shattered but not broken. You are lost.

You make me laugh. You make me cry. Everyone has secrets. You yourself have had secrets from others and still do. I have always been your secret. Was it so bad of me to not have told you mine? You who I trust implicitly. Why couldn't I tell you? Why wouldn't I tell you? Was it because I didn't want you to think any less of me? I couldn't bear to disappoint you. You who were not in my everyday life. But you who are now beginning to affect my everyday life.

Yesterday I can remember the feeling of loneliness whilst walking home after having met up with you. After I had seen you. My heart hurting. Aching. Today I am feeling both tired and weak. I couldn't and I didn't tell you yesterday. Will I be able to tell you tomorrow when we meet again? There is so much more I want to tell you. There is a possibility that I will take this secret to my grave. I can keep a secret but I am incapable of lying. It does not come instinctively at all. Possibly this is a good characteristic. I am not sure. But I can avoid telling the truth. There is a subtle difference between lying and avoiding to tell the truth.

You who could read me like a book. Still after all these years. You who could recognise from someone's body language when they were not telling the truth. I am so glad you shared that with me. But I have no need not to tell you the truth. We are not here to judge one another but to enjoy each other as we have always done.

For all these years I have lived and managed rather well with you always hidden away in the back of my mind. *Why have you come back to me now?* For what reason? To show me what has been missing from my life for all these years? Or is it to make me tell our story. Our story, which is not dissimilar to so many other people's stories. The difference being that this one belongs to us.

And tomorrow I shall see you for the last time. And after that I don't know when we'll meet again.

"The question isn't who is going to let me; it's who is going to stop me."

– Ayn Rand

"Live as if you were to die tomorrow. Learn as if you were to live forever."
– Mahatma Gandhi

THURSDAY 4 SEPTEMBER, 2014

The journey to meet you at Tottenham Court Road tube station two days later was another absolute tragicomedy. Again we had arranged to meet at 9.30am. And this time I wanted to get to the station before you. I had a spring in my step as I walked to the tube station in Hampstead. I was feeling both happy and confident. I had allowed myself plenty of time for a direct journey of only nine stops on the Northern line. And hopefully I had avoided the early morning rush hour. The train arrived within a couple of minutes and the carriage I got onto was relatively full. Looking around at the other people I wondered who they were on their way to meet, or were they just on their way to work. *What could they see about me?*

At the next station Belsize Park even more people got on and I was pleased I had a seat. Whilst the train was standing at the station platform my thoughts were abruptly interrupted by an announcement. There was a problem further along the track and the Northern line had ceased to flow. I had been so deep in thought that I hadn't noticed the train had been stationary for well over ten minutes. The doors opened and we were told to disembark. Belsize Park tube station was now closed. Trains had been cancelled until further notice.

I was in a total stupor. I couldn't believe that this was actually happening. I now needed to work out how I was going to get to Tottenham Court Road. My head was all over the place. I was at a complete loss and honestly didn't know what to do. I could barely breathe. Let alone think. We were due to meet in just over twenty minutes. I could not believe my bad luck. Every minute was precious. I did not want to be late for you.

As I fled the tube station a near miracle occurred. I saw a black cab coming down the road, its orange light burning bright. I couldn't believe my luck and without thinking I stuck out my hand and ran towards it. Simultaneously a young man had the same idea. He got to the cab first. I appeared a fraction of a second later. I begged him to share the cab with me. Sensing my obvious desperation he smiled and said yes. I knew in that moment everything was going to be alright. The cab driver dropped us both off at Goodge Street and we went our separate ways. It was a glorious day. I walked briskly down the back streets both mingling with and avoiding the masses of people. Absorbing the sights, smells and sounds of Central London. I arrived at Tottenham Court Road tube station just before you. With one minute to spare.

Whilst on my way to meeting you I had noticed a lovely café in Store Street. The café was only a short walk from the station. Surrounded by offices and hotels. The outdoor seating area had looked a bit tight with passing pedestrians, but nevertheless, I kept it in mind. The Store Street Espresso. At this point I didn't know we would be spending our precious two hours together in this café. This was the café that I would lead you back to after we had met up.

Seats were available on the pavement but you had wanted to sit inside. That had worked for me. You had led me to the back of the café and we had made ourselves comfortable on the settee. The place was empty inside. The whole café was filled with natural light from the large glass window at the front and a big skylight at the back. Right above where we sat. A cosy café with natural light is so rare to find in London. The painted white walls made the café appear bigger inside than it actually was. There was a feeling of calmness and purity in the café. You liked the coffee. It was thick and strong with plenty of life and body. Flat white. The new cappuccino. I was happy. I know how much coffee means to you. The pastries were mouthwatering. After the bustle, the noise, the people and the situations I had encountered and confronted on my disastrous journey into town, I found the Store Street Espresso the perfect antidote. *Or was it because I am with you?*

We learned a lot about each other that morning. More than some people learn in months. Maybe even years. It's quite extraordinary how different our memories are from the time we spent together. Both of us remembering totally different occasions. But equally lovely memories. Just different. You spoke about your love of surfing. Your passion. One of the reasons why you would never have been able to stay in London. Your love of the ocean. Your need to live by the sea. You had known that thirty years ago. You had said you become rather obnoxious when you are in the sea. With your surfboard. I laughed. I find this hard to imagine. I hadn't heard that word in years. Obnoxious. It took me back to my childhood. A word used to describe me at times. But you are the most gentle soul when you are on land. You are kind. You are compassionate. You are warm hearted. You have this wonderful social conscience. You understand the suffering of mistreated people. You seem to have the ability to relate to them. Are you mistreated yourself? You tell me that you love how I laugh at myself. And I tell you that I have learnt not to take myself too seriously. I can't understand a person not being able to laugh at themselves. If I don't laugh at myself then who is going to laugh with me.

I show you photos of my work. My artwork. My recycled textile art. I tell you that I haven't wanted to paint for the last couple of years. And that I don't know if I gave up painting or if painting gave me up. I am a book illustrator and a textile designer. A maker in a multitude of different disciplines. Jack of all trades. Master of none. What I lack in talent I make up for with enthusiasm. You show me some of your work. You are a photographer. Your hobby had become your career nearly thirty years ago. A successful career. Never pursuing celebrities by trying to take candid photos of them. To sell to newspapers or magazines. But a person whose creative work shows sensitivity and imagination. You talk about your work. You have amusing stories about some of the people you have photographed over the last three decades. You still do fashion shoots. You are freelance. You work for the large advertising agencies. Taking photos of food and cars also. I see from your photos how your work leans towards surrealism.

We talk about our children. Our children have grown up and are moving on with their lives. They are becoming young adults. They are the ages we were when we met in 1984, whilst we were both working at The Soho Café. Twenty-five and twenty-three years old. I enjoyed hearing what yours are up to and I enjoyed telling you about mine. We spoke about the role of being a parent. We have both encountered our own different experiences with our children. Both good and bad. Neither of us always having been totally prepared for these separate and different eventualities and experiences. But somehow managing to survive the bad ones. In time to enjoy the good ones again. Becoming an adult. A grown up can be difficult. I remember. I am trying to create happy memories for my children. You rather wisely tell me we will only stop worrying about our children when we die. You are right. And I say as a mother I am only as happy as my least happy child. We show each other photos of our children. We both remarked how good looking the other's children are. It's only when I'm back home that I realise we neither asked about nor showed each other photos of our partners. Neither of them ever having been a part of the equation. Just us. As always.

Whilst we drank our coffees and shared our pastries you told me you had recently contacted and met up with Sam. Your old friend Sam. Just before this trip to London. I was quite surprised. Sam whom you had become involved with back home after your last visit to London in 1994. Twenty years ago. The time you had come to stay with me. The last time we had seen each other. After you had sent that postcard. Looking for me. Wanting to tell me of your imminent arrival. When the new owner of our old house had called to tell me that there was a postcard for me which needed picking up. In April 1994.

I had asked why you had wanted to see Sam after all this time. Although I understood your curiosity. You had wanted to know if there was anything still there, you had replied. And there hadn't been. I had liked your answer. But it was hardly an unexpected response after all that Sam had put you through. After all that you had suffered. I thought it was rather brave of you to suggest a meet up with Sam. For many reasons. And I told you. But why after all this time I had wondered? And why just before your visit to me?

I found this interesting. Were you subconsciously coupling me and Sam? Was this some sort of coincidence? I don't think so. I'm not sure. I don't think you yourself know. I didn't ask. I will one day. What had been going on in your head? I don't like the way you appear to associate me and Sam together. I am not sure that you are aware of this. I do not like being mentioned in the same breath as Sam. I understood about you and Sam. I always have. I always will. It couldn't and wasn't going to be me. But I was the catalyst. That I know.

I asked if you had a photo of Sam. But you didn't, which wasn't really a surprise. *Why would you after all this time?* Twenty years later. You had offered to find one on the internet for me. But I had said another time. I'm not sure why I even asked. You have mentioned very little to me about Sam over the last two decades. But I remember how you suffered all those years ago. This was the first time we had spoken about Sam. Face to face. Side by side. Next to one other. The first time that we have spoken about Sam in almost twenty years. You tell me that you don't want to waste our precious time talking about Sam. And want to change the subject. That it still makes you feel uncomfortable. Sam is not a topic of pleasure for you. You don't like to be reminded about those unpleasant times. And I am glad. Because I don't want to hear any more. Just the mere mention of Sam's name brings back horrible memories for me too. I have never met Sam. I have never seen a photo of Sam. You have never described Sam to me. I have never asked you to describe Sam to me. But I have heard Sam's voice. Sam's clipped voice. I have heard Sam's hard tone. Not the same lovely drawl as you. Sam and I have spoken on the phone. The time Sam called me. Twenty years ago. The telephone conversation that I can't forget. The phone call I have never told you about. The conversation that Sam and I had in 1994. Not long before Christmas. A family time. It was during this conversation I learnt Sam was a threatening, manipulative and sly human being. A rule breaker. A would-be game changer.

We sat there in The Store Street Espresso having finished our coffees and eaten our pastries. Laughing and sharing stories. Knowing that soon we would be saying goodbye to each other. That we would be walking to Tottenham Court Road tube station together and then we would be going our own separate ways. Not knowing when we would next meet. It was hard for both of us to comprehend it had been twenty years since we had last seen each other. It felt like yesterday in many ways. Neither of us noticing that the other had aged. Although each of us noticing that we were both now wearing glasses. A sign of age. And realising how happy we were to be back in each other's company. Savouring every moment together in any which way we could. Before the inevitable goodbye. Both of us knowing we would not be waiting another twenty years until we saw each other again. That feeling still there. After all these years. And whilst we had shared many of our separate experiences I knew I wasn't going to tell you. I was not going to spoil our precious time together. I knew that you loved secrets. But I also knew that you weren't going to like this one. I knew you wouldn't like this particular secret I had kept from you. About the time when Sam had called me. Eight months after your last visit to London in 1994.

"Remember not only to say the right thing in the right place, but far more difficult still, to leave unsaid the wrong thing at the tempting moment."
– Benjamin Franklin

"Don't cry because it's over, smile because it happened."

– Dr Seuss

FRIDAY 5 SEPTEMBER, 2014

Your fleeting visit. How disappointed was I? How deeply sad. Somehow I had misunderstood or maybe I had been misinformed, but in fact you were only in town for three days. I had assumed that you were going to be in London for eleven days. Because that is what your email had said. Why had I stupidly thought that we would be able to see more of each other? I saw you twice. Twice in twenty years. That has a certain ring about it doesn't it? I had read your email correctly. Plans change. I know that. But I hadn't known that you were going to Europe with your son. And that you wouldn't be returning to London before you went back home. Perhaps that was a good thing. I had no right to be disappointed. I just hadn't spent enough time with you. I suppose I didn't want to let you go. And I suppose I never really have. I could never have enough of you. You are like a missing tooth. I can live without you. But I certainly miss you and notice your absence.

I have told you things about myself and my life that I have never told anyone else. And in particular I have spoken about my feelings. No. Not just my feelings about you. But my feelings about myself and my life. You are so very easy to talk to and I am glad that I have told you these things. You are witty and compassionate. Gentle, oversensitive and certainly good company. But then you always were. Looking into your eyes is like peering into the deep dark sea. Bottomless. What was I hoping to see there? What was I hoping to find? How can you call your partner your best friend when you have such secrets? What was I to you? How honest should one be with one's partner? Why do I often feel that I am being left behind and that life is passing me by? I've got a bad wave of missing you. The surf is catching up with me. I feel like I am drowning. I can't stop the waves. *Where are you?* I want to feel your body next to mine. Side by side. I want to touch you. But I can't.

Twice you have found me. Twice you have actively sought me out and found me since we originally met in 1984. I have never come looking for you. The first time fate intervened and we met by chance. When I swapped shifts with Charlie for the day. When you and I were both working at The Soho Café. But on opposite shifts. Thirty years ago. When we were both at a crossroads in our lives. That was the day we met by chance. On the day I swapped shifts with Charlie. As a favour for Charlie.

Why do you keep coming back to me? I'm glad that you do. We are a pendulum and a yoyo. The first time you found me was in 1994. Ten years after we had met. You came to stay. For one night only. You had taken a chance by coming to London after you had been to a convention in France. You had booked your ticket before you had even managed to contact me. I remember I couldn't have been any happier when I finally got your postcard. From the purchaser of our old house. Telling me of your imminent arrival. Approximately two weeks later. We hadn't seen each other for ten years.

And now you had sought me out again. For a second time. It is 2014 and we have just spent some very special time together in London. Twenty years have passed since we last met up. You had emailed me a couple of months ago to tell me that you were coming to London. To see your son. And of course to see me. Finally, after all these years. And now you have gone back home and I don't know when our paths will next cross. I suppose there was always going to be that moment of emptiness after we had said goodbye. That pain. I can promise you one thing, it won't be another twenty years until we see each other again.

You know what you mean to me. I recognised your soul when we met. I recognise you from my past lives. I know you were there. Perhaps we have always been separated for whatever reasons. How old is your soul? What are our reasons for not being together in this life? What happens now? You go back to your life and I happily remain in mine? We continue our parallel lives on different continents? You in America. Me in England. Until when? Still now I have more questions for you. This will always be the case I fear. But I'm not apologising. I have done enough of that already. Apologising that is.

I am that person who articulates what other people think. I asked you why you thought you had come back into my life. I liked your response. Just sticking around you had said. I never really left. Nice. Don't ever disappear. You have always been there. Lingering in the background. Hidden away but never forgotten. The same feeling for both of us. It is so comforting.

We conduct our recently renewed friendship in secret because that is what we have both chosen and want to do. I'm not sure why. A secret between a husband and wife can have a corrosive effect on a marriage. But not for mine. You are solely for me. Not to be shared. Except with Alex. Alex knows you. Alex remembers you from all those years ago. Alex remembers my other life with you. I have no secrets at all from Alex. I feel like I want to shake you. To wake you up. I want to get inside your head. You are already in mine. I have desires and passion. I am telling this story with passion. What thoughts go through your head when you think of me? What emotions do I evoke in you? You had said I was just for you. Not to be shared. With anyone. I would hate it if my husband had a friendship like this. I could not bear it if my husband had this type of friendship with another person. I would hate it if my husband had feelings for someone else like the feelings I have for you.

"The greatest happiness of life is the conviction that we are loved, loved for ourselves, or rather, loved in spite of ourselves."

– Victor Hugo

"Whatever words we utter should be chosen with care for people will hear them and be influenced by them for good or ill."

– Buddha

MONDAY 13 OCTOBER, 2014

I sit outside and drink my morning coffee. I am sheltered from the rain. I am protected by the awning. The rain is beating down on the terrace like the tears of a higher being. Somewhere. Elsewhere. I am bereft today. I miss you. Why have you told me it's a waste of my energies to miss you? That you're not worth it. You cannot tell me what to do or how to feel. Whether to miss you or not. You opened this can of worms. Or was it Pandora's Box that you opened? In the distance, I catch the sound of my neighbour's classical music playing. I hear it intermittently. It's hidden amongst the sound of the rain. And I am watching the squirrel in the tree jumping from branch to branch. Balancing like a real trapeze artist. With such total and utter dexterity. He is eating the acorns and then discarding the shells. I can hear them falling to the ground. Through the leaves. There is a large bird, a common buzzard also watching the squirrel. I am not alone in watching him. Somehow I think the buzzard and I have different interests in watching the squirrel. Mine is for pleasure. Watching his dexterity on the branches. I think the buzzard is watching with a more sinister intent. That's what it seems like to me. I miss your name not appearing in my inbox. Just a

WhatsApp please. And then it arrives. To let me know that you are thinking of me.

I know it has caught us both by surprise as to how quickly we have rekindled our friendship. When you meet someone you really connect with. There are no lines you have to say. Our connection is lasting and I believe will be truly life long. Milestone birthdays have come and gone for us both. Celebrated differently and independently. But getting to the same age. Me always first. Never the same age at the same time. The years have passed and I want you back in my life.

You tell me not to have regrets. Easier said than done. But I have so many. I feel sure most people do. In fact, my list is long. I regret the things I haven't done. Not the things I have done. The things that I couldn't control. My greatest regret is that my children never knew my father. And that neither was my father able to experience the joy of my children. I regret he never met my husband too. But I am eternally grateful that I had the chance before he died to tell him. To tell him I had met the man I was going to marry. It's easy to put someone who has died on a pedestal. But my father truly was a very special man. Held in the highest regard by so many. Even to this day. Nearly thirty years after his death. A man never to be forgotten. You and my father met in 1984. He had come over to the flat one day. Unexpectedly. When Alex and I lived together. You had been there at the time. I wonder what he would think of our recently renewed friendship. I would be interested to hear. I wonder what he thought of our friendship in 1984. I never asked him. I wasn't interested to hear then. There may be no use in regrets. But I do regret things that have been left unsaid. And I regret you. But I don't know exactly what I regret about you. I haven't worked that one out yet.

My feelings for you are so intense. There are moments in life and this is one of them. Will my feelings of emptiness ever go? It's like something is missing in my heart and soul. Unexpressed emotions are lodged in my body. But they are becoming unglued. These raw emotions which are bubbling to the surface. I desperately want to keep control and I can and I will. Skyping is like a double-edged sword. I love seeing you. I really like looking into your eyes when we talk. But I hate not being able to touch you. Sometimes after Skyping I am sad. Like today. Because what I really want to do is hug you. Really tightly. So that you can never get away. Because I know there is always more to say and I never know when that will be.

There are of course some things I didn't tell you when we met. I couldn't. And not just because our time together was so short, but because I hadn't wanted to ruin it. I have written you many lengthy emails since your recent visit. I have told you so much about myself. My innermost thoughts. The ones that are so difficult to reveal. You in turn have opened up about yourself to me. And even with your dyslexia you manage to write to me. I appreciate the effort and the time it takes you. And your lack of privacy too. There are some things I haven't told you. As I am sure there are many things you haven't told me about yourself. But this I will tell you. When we meet again. Whenever and wherever that may be. I want to hold you when I tell you. I want to feel your body next to mine. I hope you will understand why I haven't told you before now. I have never known how to tell you. I have never been able to find the right words. Or the right time.

I have discovered generally speaking that life has been good to us both. Sometimes I feel that maybe you are slightly disappointed in your work achievements. That maybe had you remained in London you would have had greater opportunities. I've seen your work. You're a very talented photographer. I remember telling you that the day you find the job you love is the day you cease to work. And you love your job. You are so passionate about your work. But you are possibly even more passionate about the ocean. I understood your decision to return home all those years ago. Swimming in the ocean is never a bad decision. There is no ocean in London. You were born to be in the sea. To gaze at it every day. To hear the waves breaking and smell the saltiness of the sea. The surf feeds your soul. You feed mine.

Recently you blasted me about my capabilities. You told me to put my creativeness to use. Why had I stopped? Why had I stopped painting? You have been trying to encourage me to write. Reminding me of that flippant remark I had made all those years ago. That one day I would write a book. Having heard and listened to both you and Alex, I have come to the conclusion that maybe you are right. I am agreeing with you both. Individually and independently you have both planted a seed in my head. I have made up my mind. I think Alex is right. Alex who is always bursting with ideas. With creativity. Alex says you are my story. That this is the story I should be telling. And you. You have told me that I should be writing a book but have never mentioned the story. I have decided I want to tell our story. Yours and mine. The story of you and me. The never-ending story.

"Words are, of course, the most powerful drug used by mankind."

– Rudyard Kipling

"If you want to keep a secret, you must also hide it from yourself."

– George Orwell

SATURDAY 15 NOVEMBER, 2014

I cannot conceal my shame. I have made numerous mistakes in my life. Admittedly no one has ever died. But they are like paper cuts to my soul. Looking back maybe I could have halted this drama from unfolding in December 1994. Eight months after your visit to me in London. Now I have the benefit of hindsight. But is that an advantage? With age too comes wisdom. I am older, stronger and wiser than I was twenty years ago. We learn from our mistakes. And we learn from our experiences. Eventually. But this wasn't my mistake. I am human through to my core. And as you yourself have said it's hard to be human on your own. Was it for me to have become involved? I can't answer that question. Even today. Although I suppose I was involved already. I know I was the catalyst.

Looking back at life through the eyes of a fifty-five year old two decades later is interesting. I wish that I could turn back the clock for you. To have been able to halt the torrent of abuse you endured for so many years. From Ashley. I knew I had unsettled you during your visit. You had left me feeling the same way. But I cannot take responsibility for what happened after you returned home. I hadn't done what you had done. I had felt neither the desire nor the need.

Sam called me early one morning. About eight months after your visit to London in 1994. Not long before Christmas. Announcing exactly who they were. A disembodied voice. Sam whom I had never spoken to before. But whom you had told me about. Sam who you were having an affair with. Your word. Not mine. An affair that had begun shortly after you had returned home from visiting me in London. Sam who you couldn't give up. Sam who had no intention of letting you go. Sam called me after having had a dreadful row with you. After you had left Sam's apartment abruptly and gone back home to Ashley. Sam had been pushing you to leave Ashley. But that was never going to happen. In your arrogance you had thought you could have them both. Sam and Ashley.

Sam had called me threatening to phone and tell Ashley about the affair the two of you were having. But even worse than that. Sam had known about the secret we had shared for so long. The secret that was yours and mine. The secret that had just been ours to share for so many years. For a decade. The secret you had kept from Ashley.

Somehow Sam had known about our secret. Sam planned to tell Ashley how you and I had deceived Ashley all those years ago. You had always denied how close our friendship had become in 1984 when we had worked together at The Soho Café. Before Ashley had arrived from Los Angeles to join you in London. Not long after you and Ashley had become engaged. At a time when I myself had been single. A long time before I had met my husband.

Sam had also known about your recent visit to me. About the detour you had taken on your way back from a convention in France. When you had come to stay with me in London. For one night only. You had not told Ashley about your visit. I remember that. We had not seen each other for ten years. But Sam knew. Why did you tell Sam? I have never asked you. Had you told Sam in a moment of weakness? I can remember what you had told me about Sam. But what had you told Sam about me? I clarified nothing in that brief telephone conversation I had with Sam.

I did try to call you once. There had been no answer. And then I forgot to call you again. I simply returned to my life. You were from my other life. I shall always feel guilty I didn't make the effort to get hold of you. There had been no answer at your house. I didn't try and call you a second time. I should have tried to call again. We lived on different continents. In different time zones. I was wrong. Maybe if I had called you would have been able to halt the drama that was about to unfold. But I didn't. I failed you as a friend. I am so sorry. Please accept my apologies. I would never intentionally want to cause you any pain whatsoever. Ever.

I am sure it would have alleviated a lot of your suffering had I called and warned you about Sam's intention to tell Ashley about the affair the two of you were having. And if I had warned you how Sam had threatened to tell Ashley about the months you and I had spent together as a couple in London, ten years earlier, at a time when you and Ashley were newly engaged. When Ashley had still been in Los Angeles. Before Ashley had joined you in London. And if I had also told you about Sam's threat to tell Ashley about your recent visit to me in London. Eight months earlier.

This was not my story. This belonged to you and Sam. And Ashley. Not me. I didn't want to be written into this chapter of your life. I had no part to play in this drama. Even today I cannot forgive Sam for having called me. For wanting to involve me. I don't know where Sam found my number. But yes, your friend Sam found it. How truly ironic that Sam managed to find my number. The one you had hidden away. The number you hadn't been able to find yourself. When you had wanted to phone and let me know of your arrival in London in April 1994.

The upset caused by having been told about us was almost too much for Ashley to bear. Confirmation of Ashley's suspicions from all those years ago.

Ashley's suspicions about us. I was the skeleton in your closet. Ashley had always been suspicious about our friendship. Yours and mine. From the first time I had met Ashley. From the first time Ashley had seen us together. Ashley wasn't stupid. Ashley I am sure has always known about you and me. I think you know that deep down too. You had tried to convince Ashley that Sam had lied. That there had never been anything between us. You knew that Ashley hadn't believed you. When Ashley had confronted you the shock on your face gave the truth away. But you stuck to your original story. As always. That nothing had ever gone on between the two of us. The story that maybe you yourself were trying to believe.

Had I called and warned you maybe you would have been able to deal with the situation before it imploded and the marriage would have stayed how it was. Safe and secure. You would not have been forced to either admit or deny Sam's words. You would have found your own words to diffuse the situation. You would have been prepared. I know how you have tormented yourself ever since. And how you have been tormented too. I know about the pain and anguish you have endured. I know how you have suffered. You have told me.

Had I called, perhaps you would have been able to avoid the breakdown in trust which plagued your marriage after Sam had made that phone call to Ashley. There were no untold secrets in your marriage. Or so Ashley had thought. Except I was your secret. And I had been your well-kept secret for over ten years. And now Ashley was questioning what other secrets there were within your marriage. After Sam made that call to Ashley the trust was gone. And the relationship became even more tense. You were given a hard time. A very hard time. For quite a few years. The affair with Sam not often discussed. But the breach of trust often thrown in your face. Ashley not wanting anyone to know of your misdemeanour with Sam. Ashley reminding you constantly of your indiscretion. Afterwards you told me Ashley hadn't been shocked by Sam's revelation that the two of you were having an affair. You and Ashley hadn't been getting on well for months. You had been an absent partner and an absent parent. Both mentally and physically. You were put on a shorter lead than we gave our dog.

Sometimes two people have to fall apart to realise how much they need to fall back together. The marriage survived. Once you realised what you could so nearly have lost. Your children, your home, your security, your life. And Ashley. Maybe it made you a better parent. Maybe it made you a better partner after the discovery of the affair. I think it probably did. Maybe my not calling enabled you to pull your marriage back together. I believe the exposure of your affair with Sam has made your marriage last until today.

But a part of you was lost in the process of surviving and rebuilding your relationship with Ashley. We hadn't spoken very often since 1994. The opportunities had been few and far between. But on the rare occasions when we had spoken it was always there. At the back of my mind. That I hadn't called you. Particularly, knowing how you had suffered, during those very difficult times when things hadn't been going so well in your life. The times you had told me about. You knew you would never have another affair. You never wanted to suffer like that again. You had told me you would never be able to endure again the guilt that came with an affair.

It breaks my heart how Ashley still rejects you. And resents you. *How could they?* Both mentally and physically. I don't understand it. I never will. Why have you subjected yourself to such misery? An affair will always be telling you something. It might mean that a couple need to break up. Or it can be a wake up call. To make a couple realise what they need to think about. Affairs can stabilise relationships. You neither complain nor do anything to improve your situation. I have asked myself time and time again why not? I don't think you know the answer yourself. I am reading between the lines and ask myself why have you resigned yourself to this state of unhappiness?

You will always be my friend. My very dear friend. My very special friend. We were never going to be together forever. *Whatever forever is?* Not in this life at any rate. Our lives had taken different paths. But this is what we had chosen. Both of us. Separately. Individually. Maybe subconsciously even together. Our communication had been limited but our friendship and that feeling had always been there. I know it will always be there too. That feeling. For both of us. Like a volcano, my memories are erupting. From my soul. They will not turn to ash. Everyone has secrets. Sometimes the secret is told and then it is no longer a secret.

"A lie can run around the world before the truth can even put shoes on."

— Mark Twain

"Words empty as the wind are best left unsaid."

– Homer

TUESDAY 23 DECEMBER, 2014

In my quiet times I like to reminisce. I am not so keen on looking at myself or seeing my reflection in the mirror. That always shocks me. Inside I feel like that young girl from the past. But now is the present. I don't look like that young girl any longer. But I still feel like her inside. As I get older I see my maternal grandmother appearing on my face. A handsome woman. I am proud to be told I look like her. I have been told that I am like her too. A strong and independent woman. I am happy about the similarities. So is my mother. Over the years I have gained different experiences of life and these show on my external body but not in my heart and soul. As I stand in front of the mirror and put my make up on I know that the mask is going on for the day. I look in the bathroom mirror. I get a shock. *Is that me?* I look so old. But in my heart and mind I am still young. There is an old saying in prison: 'Don't let your time use you. Use your time. Do something.' One of these days I'm going to wake up and look in the mirror and think *who is that old woman?* And it's going to be me. Sometimes I think, *is this what it's all about?* Surely there is more than this? More than what I ask myself.

It is Christmas time and naturally I am reminded of what I told you in your hotel room that day back in September just a few months ago. I couldn't help myself. It must have been such a shock and so hurtful. I couldn't get the words out quickly enough. They almost fell out of my mouth. I couldn't stop them. They tumbled out. Almost involuntarily. They weren't the first words I had imagined saying to you in that room. Before I had even sat down. I told you how I had come to your city in Christmas 2004. And had not contacted you. I remember the look of hurt in your eyes. I knew that look. I recognised it. From the time when you had told me all those years ago in 1984 that you were engaged. And we could never be together. I hadn't even sat down in that room when I told you.

I spent Christmas 2004 in Los Angeles. It had neither been my idea nor my choice for a family holiday destination. It hadn't been my decision at all. But I had been outvoted by the rest of my family. And I was going on holiday to the city where you lived. It had been ten years since I had last seen you. Yes, we had communicated over the years. Of course we had. But sporadically. And I had not seen you since 1994 when you had come to London for a night. When you had stayed with me. After your work convention. When you hadn't told Ashley of your detour from France to London.

I had taken the decision not to contact you in advance

of my arrival in Los Angeles. With my family. And I had decided I wasn't going to contact you when I got there either. I had been extremely anxious at the thought of coming to your neck of the woods. To be in the same city as you. Not that I knew your precise address. That wasn't relevant to me. But knowing I wouldn't be contacting you. That was really hard for me. There didn't seem any point. But my eyes would still be searching for you. I would not be able to stop looking for you amongst the crowds. To maybe catch a glimpse of you. Anywhere I went. Knowing that I could bump into you. Anywhere I might go. The possibility was always there. It would be too painful for me to see you and know that you were no longer mine and I am no longer yours. And that we couldn't be together.

I am so lucky I have Alex to talk to. I cannot bear to imagine my life without Alex. Throughout my two lives the one constant has been Alex. Alex has always been there alongside me. I have always been there alongside Alex. Alex knows it all. I know that Alex will always be on spiritual stand by for me as I am for Alex. *And you?* You have no one. That must be so hard. Why have you never told anyone about us? Although I think you did once. Sam. But that was a huge mistake. Unfortunately I think you shared our secret with the wrong person. I had discussed with Alex on numerous occasions as to whether I should contact you or not. Whether I should tell you that I was going to Los Angeles. We had unanimously agreed that I shouldn't. For a multitude of reasons. Interestingly both of us having had different reasons but coming to the same conclusion. I am not sorry about this decision I made. Even today I do not regret having not contacted you then. It was the right decision for me at that time. The time I came to your city. The time you didn't know about. I am so sorry but I wasn't up to seeing you then. I knew I wasn't strong enough to handle the situation then. You had never met my husband. And I had begun to realise I didn't want you to either. I wasn't interested in seeing Ashley. I didn't want to share you. I couldn't. You were for me as I was solely for you. And now that I was finally coming to your territory it nearly broke my heart. The thought of not being able to spend any time with you. The thought of not seeing you at all. But I had made my decision. The right decision at the right time. The years have passed since then and I am enjoying having you back in my life.

Maybe since your recent visit to London you will be able to appreciate and understand why I never contacted you when I came to your country. You have opened up this can of worms. You found me. I have never actively sought you out.

The years have passed more or less uneventfully since my family holiday to Los Angeles in 2004 with my husband and my children. The time I didn't contact you. A couple of times you told me you were trying to come to London. For work, for play. But you were a no show until September 2014. I had almost forgotten that your son was here. Well, I had put it to the back of my mind. But you. You have always been there and I know that I will never let you go. I have learned to look on the brighter side of life.

You have highlighted how hard I have become over the years. How insensitive. I have a powerful and sometimes overwhelming personality. I am too honest and that isn't a good trait. I can hurt with my honesty. But I don't mean to. I can be sweet, kind and funny too. I know you know this is true. Your manner is gentle. You are sweetly earnest. My rushed emails sometimes upset you. I know you would rather get one considered email than seven that have been rushed off. Sorry, I would never want to intentionally upset you. But please believe me that at the time of writing the email they are considered. Sometimes I think to myself I hope I don't bore you with my day-to-day life activities. Then I realise you have a choice and you only reply because you want to. Not because you have to. Now we are able to Skype. When we are alone. In our separate homes on different continents. Occasionally. Communication is so much easier. Privacy is so much harder. Why was I frightened to Skype before now? Or was it simpler then, before we had this form of communication. I tell you things that I have never told anyone else. Things that I have never spoken out loud before. I am amazed I can do this. Yet it feels so natural. Is it wise? Who knows? As long as no one gets hurt.

Please do not think of me as hard. Situations evolve and develop. There is no right or wrong. There are so many lessons to learn in life and we continue to learn all the time. We learn through our mistakes. And these mistakes in turn give us life experiences and it's these personal experiences that make each and everyone of us so unique. I have discovered and realise that we are both equally scarred and damaged from our own separate life experiences. I am damaged by events that occurred during my childhood, youth, teens and early twenties. And you are scarred by events that have happened to you.

"I've learned that people will forget what you said, people will forget what you did, but people will never forget how you made them feel"
– Maya Angelou

Honesty is more than not lying. It is truth telling, truth speaking, truth living, and truth loving."

– James E Faust

SUNDAY 18 JANUARY, 2015

Outside I can see the snowdrops beginning to break through the frozen soil. Snowdrops marking the first sign of spring. They are very early this year. Flowering ahead of daffodils and bluebells and then of course the tulips, which will eventually erupt into a mass of colour. I planted the tulips when you were here. Here in my city but sadly not on my terrace.

At fifty-five years old I am almost invisible. But not to you. And although I like to dress in a riot of colour I am very much a black and white person. There is no grey area for me. What you see is what you get. I have been told at times I can be like a steamroller. I have been told at times I have no filter. I never mean to offend.

The intensity of our friendship can be overwhelming. I have realised we share something very special. This is so precious. You evoke something in me that is too impossible to express. To put into words. You have resurrected feelings and emotions I had forgotten even existed. You have reignited the feelings of both passion and desire within me. I don't know how I would ever describe this friendship. We are very close friends and on occasions that friendship has gone too far. Our friendship had developed into intimacy many years ago. I can remember it like it was yesterday. Don't be scared by my certainty and focus.

Why do I detect a sense of disappointment in your communication to me about certain aspects of your life? Or is that my imagination? This morning you were in a mood. You had said that sometimes you couldn't figure out what the point of our existence was, which makes you angry. It happens from time to time. More so as you get older. This mood was set off by looking at your wetsuit dry. Knowing that one day you won't be able to surf any more. You had asked me if you were full of only nothing but grumpiness at the moment. There are constant changes in my life. The weather. My mood. The seasons. The time. Your mood. Fashion. Technology. *Shall I go on?* But not my feelings for you. Those have never changed.

You tell me you think you are spending too much time Skyping and talking to me at the moment. But that you are enjoying it. Please don't feel this way. Carry on enjoying the moment. I am. You, who so clearly live in the moment. I'm not asking anything from you but simply enjoying your company. You also say that one day we'll have to cut back on this amount of communication. That we couldn't possibly keep up the momentum. I'm not sure why. Well, that you wouldn't be able to because life gets crazy sometimes. I wasn't sure what that really meant. Now

I am learning this means a complete and utter lack of privacy at your end. There are other reasons too. But I haven't worked out what these are yet. There will be times when we can and times when we can't. Let's make the most of when we can. And then you say you feel like I will always be there and that this is a great feeling. And I told you that it's also true.

If I thought there was the faintest chance of you coming round to my home right now I would be hanging out of my window waiting for you. Anticipating your arrival with excitement. But instead I keep the mobile next to me. Waiting for the signal that we can go ahead and continue our discovery of each other. You have begun to unlock my deepest secrets. I have revealed some of my most innermost thoughts to you. We send each other copious amounts of emails and WhatsApps. The first thing I do when I wake up in the morning is to check if I have heard from you. Something. Anything. A WhatsApp, an email. Even just two kisses. A signal that you are thinking about me. Very occasionally there is even a photo. Not often of you but always a photo that manages to put a smile on my face. A grin at other times. Sometimes you WhatsApp giving me a time for a possible Skype conversation. And if there is nothing from you I am sad. But I am learning to deal with that feeling.

Because I know it doesn't mean that you're not thinking about me. I know that I am very much on your mind and in your thoughts. I will always be there for you. You are right. As I know you will always be there for me. As I have said before, I hold a very special place in my heart just for you. It's been there a long time. It will never go away if it hasn't up to now. And besides, I don't want it to.

The similarities in our lives are incredible. Separate experiences. Living on different continents. In different countries. In different cities. You in Los Angeles. Me in London. But the same soul. Married to other people. Both of us in marriages that have given us what we want and need. Our words. Security, stability, love, friendship and children. The past another life. Over the years I have at times entertained the thought of what would have been if we had pursued a life together. I have a wonderful life but something is missing from it. I know that something is you. And I am not quite sure where you fit in my life. That is, of course, if you do at all. I know we have been together before. I know we will be together in another life. I cannot answer about this one. I know that eventually we will be together. I just don't know in which life.

"Open your eyes, look within. Are you satisfied with the life you're living?"
— Bob Marley

"Nothing ever becomes real till it is experienced."
— John Keats

THURSDAY 19 FEBRUARY, 2015

Today I am wearing one of the outfits I wore when we last met. I like to wear the clothes I wore when I saw you. Even though they have been washed many times since then. And I am also not exactly sure about which scarf I wore. Wearing these clothes makes me feel close to you. I don't know why. Do you feel the same way about the clothes you wore? I think about how we both arrived wearing backpacks. And of course we now both wore glasses. The exact same ones but in different colours. What a pair. So very similar in so many ways and probably very different in others. But I am less aware of our differences.

I cannot believe we never set eyes upon each other for twenty years. And now if I don't hear from you on a regular basis I am sad. You have restored my belief in myself. You heal me. You continue to inspire me. You feed my creativity. I am like a bottomless pit where you are concerned. You are my fantasy. My muse.

I have told you I like the person you have grown into, which worries you a bit. You suspect because I don't know you that well and that you don't really have a high opinion of yourself. That upset me. The fact that your self-esteem is low. I wonder why this is.

Although I know verbal bullying and humiliation has certainly had an impact on your self-esteem. I know you are particularly sensitive about your dyslexia. If you were to ask me have I grown up, developed and matured into the person you thought I would become, my answer to you would be yes. You are exactly how I always imagined you would be and more. My question to you is *am I the person you thought I would become?* Although I think I know the answer to this question. I remember how I could never have enough of you then. I feel the same way now. *What do I do for you?* Tell me please. I think I know. I am beginning to know you better now. Better than I did a few months ago. Better than I did all those years ago. Unfortunately, I can't remember too well what we used to talk about when we were in our twenties. But I do know this. I liked you then and I still like you now. Maybe even more so now as I appreciate the person you have become. Our mutual respect and deep affection growing as we learn more about each other.

Just because I have stopped myself from doing so many things in my life I am not going to stop this friendship. I can count the number of true friends I have on one hand. I wonder how I ever let you go. And then I remember you gave me no choice. I do not regret the years of so little contact between us. I am not allowed regrets. I have lived my life for so long without you in it. What you gave me then, you continue to give me now. But you have now become one of those friends who I like to have contact with every day. Except with you I can't. I have to wait for you to tell me the coast is clear. We pre-book times in the hope that we will be able to follow through with a Skype chat on that chosen date. But often they can't go ahead. These chats don't happen enough. They can't. They are too few and far between. Sometimes it's a matter of weeks until we can Skype again. And at the moment I am enduring one of these periods. Sometimes we can speak once a week for a month, and then not get the opportunity for another month after that. That's the way it is.

I have begun to realise you get very little privacy at home. I cannot comprehend this. But Alex has explained to me that my life is the abnormal one. Not yours. Originally I hadn't wanted to Skype you. And now when we do and my screen freezes it is torture. What am I missing now? What am I missing all the time? I have lost so many moments in these lapses. I ask you to repeat yourself. Not wanting you to feel distracted by the technical glitches fragmenting your story. Reminding me of the thousands of miles that keep us separated. I want you to speak to me as if I'm in the same room as you. Right next to you. Side by side. Maybe it's for the best that we can't Skype too often. And not just because it seems difficult for you to get the time alone. I must stop checking my phone waiting for your name to appear via any form of communication. Now, as I am alone at home and checking my phone, I wonder if this is all in my imagination. My memories of being with you have faded. But not the feeling.

I don't remember the transitional period between my two lives. I can't recall the final moments of my last life. The life I shared with you. I don't remember saying goodbye to you. I have never been able to. Neither can I recall the beginning of my new life. The life I share with my husband. The life you are not a part of. I am not good at letting go of things. Or at saying goodbye. But we both know that. And neither are you. You always run from me. I have learnt it isn't because you don't want to stay with me, it's because you have to leave. Always.

"Ultimately, you have to pursue your own path, not someone's idea of the right path. You need to stay on your path."

– Baz Luhrmann

"There is a wisdom of the head, and there is a wisdom of the heart."

– Charles Dickens

MONDAY 9 MARCH, 2015

My loneliest times are at night when I can't sleep. I think of you whilst listening to my husband's rhythmic breathing and tonight I can hear the hoot of an owl. The wise owl. Calling me. The owl who is often associated with intuition and clairvoyance. The owl who penetrates the darkness of the blackest night. Seeing and hearing what others can't. What can he see and hear that I can't? I think he wants me to listen to the wisdom that is deep in my heart and soul. He is trying to help me. To reach me in the current challenge that I am facing. I think he is telling me to open my eyes and my ears as well as my mind to see the truth of the situation. There is something I need to see and hear. *What indeed is the truth?* I don't know any more. Maybe his wisdom will come to me when I am sleeping. In my dreams. The owl is a messenger that can bring clarity. *What is the message that he has for me?*

Sometimes I go outside and look at the moon and think of you. On the flipside. Far away but always in my heart. My husband goes to work unbearably early. Often I cannot go back to sleep. Then I start to think. In these quiet moments. I think of you. I think about you endlessly. I spend an enormous amount of time thinking about you. At different times of the day and night. Probably too much time. But I can't help myself. My mind tends to wander. It seems I am able to retrieve more memories from those happy times we shared together than I had originally thought.

And sometimes I think about what could have been. And then I think that is ridiculous. And then I realise that we all have choices and that we all make our own choices. In life you have choices and choices have consequences. Destiny is destiny. But ultimately, we all choose our own paths and that does not always mean following our true destiny. You get a pack of cards dealt to you at the beginning of life but you can always switch your hand. I have never seen you in my past lives but I know you were there. Perhaps we have always been separated for whatever reasons. But I recognised your soul when we met.

What really were our reasons for not being together? Sometimes I feel my life could have taken a different path. Maybe I should be writing about what could have happened. What would have happened if I had followed the other path? Sometimes I wonder why I am who I am and how did I get to this point. If I am totally honest with myself, I don't feel my life could have been any other way. I try not to have any regrets. I try and remind myself of this. I had buried you away for so long. You have always been there at the back of my mind. I had boxed you up and hidden you away.

What a debacle. I am totally immersed in these feelings you have resurrected within me. These feelings that I have for you. Still after all these years. You make me think about and remember things that have disappeared from my life. You may not think I have changed but in many ways I have. And for this at times I feel sad. You remind me of a different life. I think of you wantingly, knowingly, lovingly. Remembering you always. Thinking of you so often. I have never wanted to be perfect. Whatever perfect is? Not everyone is perfect. The perfect life does not exist. If people think it does they are untrue to themselves. Not everything is as perfect as it seems.

What is one of our main concerns? That one of us will die and the other won't know. We share the same fear of not knowing if something happens to the other. How will we find out? I know that Alex will let you know if I am in need. Sometimes I panic and think that something will happen to you and I will never see you again. It makes me anxious. Who will tell me if you need me and you cannot let me know yourself? I shall have to rely on my sixth sense. You have been such an integral part of my life. And still are. Always there. Not next to me but always in my heart. Spiritually by my side. I often wonder what you would think of some of my actions but I generally don't get the chance to discuss them with you until the time has passed. Opportunities to talk so few and far between. Particularly as you don't like speaking on the phone. Maybe this is a good thing.

I have so much I want to tell you. I have so much I want to ask. I have realised the privacy you get at home is minimal. It isn't the time difference that makes it so difficult for us to communicate. It is your lack of privacy at home. I love it when you work away from home. Then there are no restrictions on our contact. I don't like not being able to speak to you whenever I want. Maybe this is what being in prison feels like. My own internal prison. I hope you won't be under house arrest when I arrive.

Sometimes it's really hard to have a conversation with you. Between the time difference and the deletion of WhatsApps and emails, I seem to lose the thread of a particular conversation. I don't always know what's going on. And neither do you. It can become confusing and frustrating for both of us. But not today. Today we are answering each other's questions. Or you are answering mine at any rate. Sometimes I feel you are selective about which questions of mine you choose to answer. I also know writing isn't easy for you and that some questions require short answers and others much longer ones. But you have told me that you will answer any question I have for you. That I can always ask you anything I like. I was overwhelmed by that remark. The level of intimacy within our friendship runs very deep indeed. I am just for you.

You have told me that it's weird and rather disturbing, but when you've been thinking about something for a few days, I pop up and verbalize your thoughts. And that it happens often. Likewise. The same happens to me. I check my WhatsApp constantly. And I have begun to notice that at the moment of my checking I can see you have either been online a minute or two beforehand. Or even more coincidentally, you are often typing me a message at the precise moment when I am gazing at your name. We are very much in tune with each other. We always have been. We always will be. You are a distraction. From what I do not know.

"It is not in the stars to hold our destiny but in ourselves."

– William Shakespeare

"In any moment of decision, the best thing you can do is the right thing, the next best thing is the wrong thing, and the worst thing you can do is nothing."

– Theodore Roosevelt

THURSDAY 16 APRIL, 2015

This morning I woke to the plaintive call of the cuckoo. Not a bird you hear very often. But the bird who announces spring. And whilst listening to the cuckoo I remembered how as a child I would be encouraged to make a wish on hearing the first cuckoo call of the season. The wish which supposedly would always come true. Today whilst hearing the cuckoo I have made my wish. I think you know what it is. And just in case you don't I shall tell you. My wish is to come and see you. The cuckoo is also a symbol of infidelity and selfishness. The bird who lays her eggs in another bird's nest. Apparently, only people suffering from pain will understand the cuckoo's song. I question whether I understand her song or not. But this morning whilst listening to her I had a moment of clarity.

I am lucky enough to enjoy both the luxury of personal space and time. I am able to think, to remember, to reminisce and to write down my thoughts. These ever changing thoughts. Only the feeling remains the same. You are becoming a part of my everyday life. I'm not quite sure how and where you fit into it though. Whilst I work I daydream and I think of you. How can I allow myself to think of you so often? Where do all these thoughts and memories come from? They have been locked away. For so many years. But it hasn't been hard to retrieve them. Why would it be? I have come to a decision. I want to come and visit you. I am not sure any longer what is real and what is in my imagination. Help me please. I know you can. I also know you will.

I had wanted to tell you face to face on Skype about my very exciting news. About my thoughts. My proposed idea. So that I could have seen your immediate and true response to what I was about say. I like to look deeply into your eyes when I ask you questions or tell you something. Especially when it is something of such importance. And in this particular instance I really wanted to capture that reaction shot in real time. This was definitely a Skype conversation. But there hadn't been an opportunity over the last couple of weeks. We had both been busy working. Our individual schedules weren't enabling us to find the time and in your case the privacy. I was desperate to talk to you. To tell you my idea. I didn't know when the next opportunity to speak would be. This of course wasn't unusual. But I was dying to tell you. I couldn't contain myself any longer. Because I wanted you to know. And I wanted you to know almost as soon as I had known myself. So I wrote you an email:

SURPRISE! I'M COMING TO YOUR PART OF

THE WORLD. WELL SUBJECT TO YOUR APPROVAL OF COURSE?! HOW DOES THAT SOUND? I'LL BE ARRIVING ON JUNE 6. I HOPE YOU'LL BE AROUND? I'M WILLING TO TAKE THE CHANCE! I THINK THIS IS A SKYPE CONVERSATION. X

This is something I really want to do. I want to come to your city. I want to see you in your hometown. In Los Angeles. This time I am giving you both the option and the opportunity of meeting up. Both the option and the opportunity that I never offered you ten years ago during the Christmas period of 2004 when I was there. When I never contacted you. When I was in Los Angeles with my husband and my children on a family holiday. I feel like I have to see you again. I want to see you again. I almost need to see you again. I am almost obsessed with the idea. But I am running it by you first. Before I confirm my ticket. I hadn't seen you for twenty years. Those two days in London hadn't been enough. Our time together had been so brief. I knew you felt the same way.

I have come to realise that whilst writing this story—our story—there is always more to say. You had left my life as quickly as you had come back into it. I am almost on my way. My ticket is booked. But not confirmed. I would never be so brave as to confirm the booking without asking you first. About your thoughts. Should I come and visit you. *Would you like me to?* Perhaps you won't want me to, although I hoped this wasn't the case.

You replied to my email almost immediately, which is quite unlike you. But I knew you would. To this particular one. I know you rather well. You seem to know me rather well too. Your response was quite terse:

HEY GIRLIE,
YOU CERTAINLY KNOW HOW TO THROW A CURVE BALL. IF YOU'RE IN TOWN I'D BE VERY SURPRISED IF I DIDN'T GET TO SEE YOU. AT LEAST FOR A FEW HOURS HERE AND THERE. BUT THE PROBLEM IS THAT THERE CAN BE NO GUARANTEES. YOU ARE COMING DURING MY VERY BUSY PERIOD. I COULD BE WORKING AWAY. I OFTEN DON'T KNOW MY SCHEDULE UNTIL VERY LATE IN THE DAY. YOU'RE RIGHT. THIS IS A SKYPYE CONVERSATION. MAYBE TONIGHT I'LL HAVE TIME.
XX

I could tell by your immediate response that you weren't overly shocked by my email. I hadn't really thought you would be either. But you seemed surprised. I could tell the difference between shock and surprise. I wasn't upset by your blunt reply to me. Reading between the lines I could sense your fear. I think I also knew why. But you were wrong. You had nothing to be worried about.

Because my reply to you was so unlike anything I would normally write, I can remember smiling to myself as I wrote it:

NOT QUITE SURE WHAT TO WRITE SO BEST I SAY NOTHING. LOOK FORWARD TO SKYPING WHENEVER YOU CAN. X

Something Alex had taught me over the years. When in doubt say nothing. But at the time of writing I really hoped we would be able to Skype in the not too distant future. One never knew. But what I did know was that if you couldn't meet up with me or didn't want to, I would fully understand. A moment of truth. I would be absolutely devastated if I didn't get to spend some quality time with you. I was eager to talk to you as soon as possible. I had only mentioned about the possibility of coming to visit you. I hope this made sense to you. It did to me.

And very shortly after I had replied to your email, I received another one from you:

SO HAPPY YOU'RE COMING OVER HERE. I'LL BE DOING ALL I CAN TO SPEND SOME MEANINGFUL TIME WITH YOU. I SO WANT TO SHOW YOU AROUND MY HOOD. I DON'T WANT TO TELL ASHLEY YOU'RE COMING.

YOU'RE FOR ME. NOT TO BE SHARED. SERIOUSLY HAPPY.
XX

The email I had wanted to receive and the one I knew spoke the truth. The one that had almost made me cry with happiness. The email I had hoped to get and the one that I knew would eventually come. The email telling me that you wanted to see me. The email telling me you were really happy with my idea. I thought you would be after the initial shock. The email that had led to a really emotional Skype conversation. I can't wait to see you. To stand next to you. I only want to dance with you. Like we used to when we met. All those years ago. Thirty years ago. In 1984 when we both worked at The Soho Café. I want to dance with you again so that we may hold each other and feel the music. I have enjoyed listening to the lyrics of the songs you have recently been sending me. Although I don't always appreciate the music. Sometimes I hear songs on the radio that take me back to when we were together. Our taste in music may differ. But our taste for each other is the same. I can't wait to see you. I feel really calm and happy about coming to visit. I am smiling at the thought of laughing with you.

I think we both knew in our heart of hearts this was going to happen. I think we both subconsciously knew that this was on the cards. I feel like this is my one shot and I'm taking it. It has to be this way. It was you who said we have to enjoy the good times and make the most of every opportunity. And this is exactly what I have decided to do. I am taking this opportunity to enjoy a good time with you. That's right isn't it? That is what you have said about life. We have to enjoy the good times and make the most of every opportunity. I am giving us both this opportunity.

I want you to take me somewhere new. I want you to take me with you. Somewhere you haven't been before. To a place just for us two. Where I can hear the roar of the surf and feel the sand between my toes. And be with you. Just you. So that I may hold your body close to mine. Let me make you happy. Let me look into your eyes and let me touch your soft skin. Let me get to know you. Let me get into your head if I am not there already. For you are in mine. Take me to that special place. Wherever that may be.

Over the years I have learned there is absolutely no point in pre-empting a situation. Whichever way you think the game will play out it doesn't. I have spent countless wasted hours imagining and expecting the worst possible scenarios. Only to be pleasantly surprised. As you know I like to look on the bright side of life and today I can really feel that brightness shining down on me. Alex has told me it is a very big gesture I am making by coming out to see you.

I am impatient with greed. I want to savour every moment with you. My appetite for you has always been insatiable. I am like a dog with a bone where you are concerned. I cannot and will not let you go. Not now. Not again. You know I don't give up. On anything. I never have. And never will. That just isn't me. In a different life who knows what could or may have been. But in this life this is the situation that we are in. I want to see you in real time. Face to face. So that I may hold you. So that I may touch you and feel you next to me. So that I may stroke your very soft skin.

"We dance round in a ring and suppose, but the secret sits in the middle and knows."
– Robert Frost

"A brain of feathers, and a heart of lead."
– Alexander Pope

TUESDAY 12 MAY, 2015

Recently I have been finding feathers around the house. Not one but three in the last month. First, I found a little white feather by the kitchen sink. Then another larger one a week or so later in the hall. Also white in colour. Yesterday, I found a much larger one, half grey and half white. I believe my angel is trying to tell me something. And as the feathers get larger in size and the colour changes I wonder what the actual message is I am being given. An answer to which particular question of mine. I have so many. White being the symbol of faith and protection. Grey and white telling me what? Grey being a very neutral colour but the other half of the feather pure white. Why do I get the feeling my father is trying to tell me something? What is the message that he is trying to send me? To get me to understand what? I wonder what my father would think about our renewed friendship. You met each other once. All those years ago. In 1984. Which particular question is my father responding to? I don't know if I am even asking him any questions. I know I am questioning myself. From wherever he may be my father is always with me. I know that he is guiding me.

Your email came like a bolt of thunder. Out of the blue. Twelve hours after a really lovely Skype conversation. One of many we had recently enjoyed. I am sure that's why. Over the last few days we had been chatting regularly. You were working in a different city for a week or so. Far from home. But also further away from me. We had taken full advantage of this situation. Both of us continuing to appreciate our ongoing rediscovery of each other. Your hotel room had become your temporary home. You were empowered by your freedom. And I was benefiting from this newfound privilege. Or so I had thought:

I CAN'T DO THIS. ALL THE FEELINGS OF GUILT, DISHONESTY, BETRAYAL AND HURT ARE COMING BACK TO ME. YOU'VE NO IDEA HOW BAD IT CAN MAKE YOU FEEL. THE THING I HATED ABOUT THAT TIME WAS I ULTIMATELY HURT TWO PEOPLE WHO I THOUGHT A LOT ABOUT. AND I THINK THIS WILL HAPPEN AGAIN. I DON'T WANT TO PLAY WITH YOUR EMOTIONS. OR MINE. OR ASHLEY'S. I'M JUST TOO OLD AND TIRED FOR THAT.
XX

Your email is one long cry of pain. What depths of hopelessness, despair and sadness are contained in it. Mental and imaginative infidelity is real. There is no self-pity but I feel your torture. *What had happened to the person I thought I knew so well?* What were you panicking about? Suddenly you have become overtaken with guilt. And I'm not quite sure why. I am overcome with sadness. This is an intense friendship. But not a betrayal. We both have different concerns about my forthcoming visit. But please remember: I am not Sam. I would never want to make you feel badly about yourself. You had resurrected our friendship. I didn't share your guilt. I wasn't the one who had been engaged when we had spent those very special times together. All those years ago in 1984. Before I had met my husband. I had been single. You had been engaged. You were from the life I had lived before I was married. My other life. I didn't have to feel any of those emotions. I had also never had an affair.

Your WhatsApp came through literally minutes after that email. The email I hadn't known how to respond to. The email you fortunately hadn't given me time to respond to. The email I think you may have even regretted sending:

CAN YOU SKYPE NOW? I WANT TO BE YOUR FRIEND. I LOVE BEING YOUR FRIEND. I LOVE CHATTING TO YOU. I LOVE HOW DAFT YOU CAN BE. I LOVE HOW YOU LAUGH AT YOURSELF. YOU REALLY ARE ONE OF A KIND. I HAVE TO TALK TO YOU.
XX

Breathe. As you always say to me. Breathe. You were firing shots from two directions. Different thoughts.

Different people. Different outlook. Different concerns. I could sense the urgency in your tone of writing. You had to talk to me. You wanted to Skype right now. If possible. We Skyped immediately. Thank goodness I check my email and my WhatsApp continuously.

During that Skype conversation you told me you loved how good, open and honest our friendship was. You told me the level of intimacy we had achieved went beyond and far deeper than any physical intimacy you had recently enjoyed. You told me you didn't want us to suffer. Neither of us. I agreed that talking openly and honestly was one of the most intimate acts of all. I also said I felt the level of honesty and intimacy we had resumed in our friendship and shared together went far deeper and superseded any physical relationship we could ever have or enjoy together again. The meeting of two souls. You had said that I was probably right actually and you hated it when you agreed with me sometimes. The pleasure and exhilaration of the affair was paid for in the agony you suffered by having caused so much pain. To all three of you. Particularly Ashley. And you had indeed told me about those feelings.

I didn't understand your panic. I didn't understand your guilt. You told me how our friendship was beginning to bring back memories and feelings you associated from the time when you were with Sam.

Feelings of self-hatred, deceit and mistrust. How you had hurt two people who you had cared about very much. I told you to clear your head. I told you I thought perhaps you had hurt three people during that period. That maybe you had forgotten to include yourself. You told me I was very wise for one so daft. I can't control your feelings but I can stop the contact between us.

You are so damaged from the affair you had over twenty years ago. For which I have always felt somewhat responsible. Your guilt and fear stronger and clearer than the look of sorrow in your eyes. Your behaviour is repetitive. It always has been. You send a long email telling me about your feelings of guilt about our friendship. And that you want to cut back on contact. And then a few hours later a pleading WhatsApp. *Will I call you? Or can I text you?* That you miss me. You always come back to me. You confuse me. You are confused yourself. You have never really wanted to let go. Your words. Not mine. You have suffered a gruelling and emotional payback that has continued since your affair was disclosed. Since you saw the devastation on Ashley's face on hearing about both your affair with Sam and about us. Sam told Ashley about the relationship we had enjoyed before Ashley had joined you in London thirty years ago, when you and Ashley had been engaged.

I would never want to hurt you, myself or our partners. I don't like the idea that I am causing you discomfort in any shape, form or manner whatsoever. I don't want to mess with your head. I don't want to cause you pain. Or distress. Please just go with the flow and know that I can't wait to see you. That's all. Just to have a good laugh with a very special friend. No terms. No conditions. Just the mutual respect that we share for one another. You had said that was a nice thing to say. What we had was then. And this is now. A different time. The same two people living separate lives with different partners. But always the feeling. Where has my friend with the half-full glass disappeared to? I know you suffered all those years ago and during the ensuing years also. But this is not the same. Again, I must remind you. I am not Sam. I am not Ashley. You are bruised. You are scarred. You are lost.

There have been times when I myself have struggled but I have come to terms with the conventionality of my life. Slipping into an easier life meant abandoning a part of myself. My husband often interrupts my thoughts and tells me to look forwards and not backwards. Perhaps he is right. *You started this.* Again you found me. After having sought me out. When you came to London last year. To see your son. And me. I think you are beginning to understand why I never contacted you when I came to your neck of the woods during the Christmas period of 2004. Why have I always been that one step ahead of you? Even then and most definitely now.

I have asked you a few times. I certainly don't want to put more conflicting thoughts or ideas into your head. To confuse you even more. But I have asked if you truly want me to come and visit. You have told me that you do. You are very honest. I respect your brevity and honesty in certain things you have told me. I respect your fears and your concerns. The fears and concerns that you have for both of us. I respect your sense of responsibility. You have told me enough times. I am now convinced you want me to come and visit you. Please know I have no expectations, and I can truly and honestly say that you could never disappoint me in any way at all. Just don't get hurt. I wouldn't want that for either of us. But particularly not for you. Not again.

You tell me you are selfish and do not want to share me. I say that's not selfish at all. The way it was. The way it is. The way it will always be. I tell you that I want to see you again in real time. To touch you. To feel you next to me. To hold you in my arms. Like we used to. All those years ago. I hope this makes sense to you.

I never feel like I have to pretend with you. I only want to tell you the truth. I don't feel the need to withhold anything from you. I can be myself with you. You recognise my strengths and my weaknesses.

You don't judge me or define me by my errors and shortcomings. You take me at face value. For whom I am and what I stand for. I want to know more about you and don't know where to start. I share my life with my husband but I want to share my innermost thoughts and feelings with you.

"I find hope in the darkest of days, and focus in the brightest. I do not judge the universe."
– Dalai Lama

"If you want a happy ending, that depends, of course, on where you stop your story."

— Orson *Welles*

SATURDAY 6 JUNE, 2015

Your part of the world is far away from mine and my journey is about to begin. Well, actually it began a year ago. I will be arriving in Los Angeles exactly a year to the day since I received your email telling me of your trip to London. It will also be nine months since we last met up, after not having seen each other for twenty years. The length of a pregnancy. The time it takes to bring a new life into this world. I did tell you then that it wouldn't be another twenty years until we met again. This morning when I was making coffee I had to pinch myself. I am not quite sure how this trip of mine came to be. Who indeed planted the seed? I can't answer that question. But I do know it is an opportunity I am taking with both hands.

I am exhilarated at the prospect of spending time with you. I have been thinking back, reminiscing and remembering how this past year has developed and how it has taken me to where I am now. Sitting on a plane. Sending you a text saying:

I'M ON MY WAY. X

Sometimes you have to fly a very long way to get to where you really are. In your head. Where you really want to be. In your body. I have begun to understand and accept that the feeling will always be there. Forever. For both of us. That this feeling has never left in thirty years. For either of us. That it has always been there from the beginning. And that it will be there until the end. For both of us. That because this feeling has never gone. It never will. And I remind myself whilst sitting here on the plane that we both chose the way we live our lives. But I don't remember the reasons for having made these choices. By either of us.

The plane is pushing back. Before taxiing to the runway. I want the captain's welcoming announcement to be over, so that I can enjoy the silence. I want to be alone with my thoughts. My thoughts of you. The plane is being pulled forward to straighten up. I look around at the other passengers surrounding me. Their voices have subsided. The introductions and pleasantries almost over. They have settled down. I scrutinise the expressions on their faces. Mine is hidden away behind my scarf. But surely they can see the tremendous excitement in my eyes? What are their reasons for making this very long journey? The safety demonstration has now started. The plane has come to a standstill. Who are the other passengers going to meet? What are their expectations? If any. I'm interested to know their stories. So many thoughts. So many questions. Always. The safety demonstration has ended. The engines are turning. I have switched off my phone. My seat belt is on and I am locked in. Both in my seat and with the promise of seeing you. It doesn't seem real. My dream is about to become my reality.

Tapestry is a simple, repetitive and oddly satisfying task that clears my head. It has a soothing and hypnotic effect, which calms my mind. I like to stitch. I find it therapeutic. Relaxing. And this is how I choose to pass the time on the long flight, which is exhausting but not uncomfortable. And when my eyes begin to tire I close them, and my thoughts return to you whilst I try to fall asleep. When I think of you I do so with such deep affection.

I am woken very suddenly. There is severe turbulence. The flight path is very bumpy. Up and down. Up and down. As is the path of life itself. Suddenly, I can feel myself being thrown about. Both physically and mentally. And it isn't fun. I hoped this wasn't a sign of times ahead. Was this another warning? And if so from whom? And what was I being warned about? I hoped these abrupt jolts weren't significant. That they weren't an indication as to how our time together would unfold. I smiled and laughed to myself as I thought back to our past reunions. They certainly hadn't evolved as planned. Either of them. But neither had they been disappointing. Either of them. After a last few tremors the turbulence was over. An air of calm returned to the cabin. And whilst my thoughts returned to you I drifted off back to sleep for the remainder of the flight.

The years of friendship and the long distance between us have enabled us to see each other as individuals. We are two souls disconnected from any reality. We hold onto each other to feel that sense of belonging. We will meet in secret. Our friendship will always remain a secret because this is what we have both chosen. We share a connection. A private intimate connection. This trip I hope will offer me a renewed sense of anonymity. The same anonymity I enjoyed when working at The Soho Café. Perhaps I can only be anonymous when I am with you.

The plane has landed. And I have switched on my phone. I am not allowing my mind to wander to the future or the past. I am grounded. I am in the present. There is a definite flutter of excitement around. And I am absorbing the moment. The doors have been opened. There is a certain frisson in the air. I have unwound my scarf. And I am breathing in your air. Deep, slow, long breaths. To combat my racing heart. My phone vibrates. There is a message from you:

SO HAPPY. SERIOUSLY HAPPY. XX

"Buy the ticket, take the ride."
– Hunter S Thompson

ABOUT THE AUTHOR

Lynda Young Spiro is a mixed media artist whose love of textiles, found objects and recyclable materials are incorporated into her colourful work. Lynda was born in 1959 in Hampstead, London, where she now lives with her husband and two sons. Lynda's previous book *Latch-Hooking Rugs* is published by A & C Black. *There is Always More to Say* is her first novel.

www.thereisalwaysmoretosay.com
www.lyndaspiro.com